Cowboy BAD Boys

by Randi Alexander

Body Heat – When a rancher and his gorgeous passenger are buried in his truck under an avalanche, they discover a sensual way to keep warm.

Breakfast in Bed – A ranch foreman devises a plan to keep his woman from bolting out of his bed every time they're through making love.

Hard Headed Cowboy – When a rodeo bull rider needs a lift, his sexy equipment sponsor makes him a proposition.

High Country Ride – Fulfilling her father's last wishes, a city girl hires a hot cowboy to guide her into the Rockies.

Kill Me or Kiss Me – With her life in danger, an exotic dancer has to trust a sexy cattle rustler to keep her alive.

No Way Out – The town sheriff and the beautiful bank president he's been lusting after are cornered by a killer.

Private Lessons – When her girlfriends buy her a mechanical bull lesson with a real bull rider, a college girl gets a sensual ride from her high school crush.

Stubborn Redhead – The rancher's woman left him because of rumors of his cheating, but what will it take to make her believe his innocence?

Takin' a Chance – A barrel racer has one last opportunity to seduce the sexy rodeo bullfighter she's fallen for.

Where We Left Off – In desperate need of help, a country veterinarian contacts the man she'd loved but booted out of her life years ago.

Cowboy Bad Boys

Ten Erotic Romances

By Randi Alexander

Edited by Sky Robinson and Ursula Avery

ISBN: 978-1470067700

STORIES

Body Heat

Micah Blain set down the newspaper and pulled his ringing cell phone out of his coat pocket. "Blain."

"Hi, Micah?" a breathless female voice asked. "It's Destiny."

He grinned. *Destiny calling? Too ironic.* "Are you here?" He looked at the list of arriving flights on the airline's display behind him. Hers had finally landed at 1:46 AM. Three hours late due to the snow.

"I'm just walking into the..." Their eyes met across the nearly empty room. She lowered her phone and walked toward him.

He stood and pulled his black Stetson from his head. Well, hell. She was a looker. Short brown hair ending in a straight line just below her ears. A heart-shaped face and the sweetest set of red lips he'd ever wanted to kiss.

Hauling her suitcase behind her, she walked on shiny black high-heeled boots, her black pants tucked into them. Long, thin legs. Slim hips. Her small breasts showed round and firm under her red turtleneck. Tracy had mentioned she was a model. He could definitely see it.

She stopped in front of him, nearly as tall as his six feet, two inches in those nasty heels. He'd like to feel them poking into his ass as he pumped into her. He swallowed, blinked, and took the hand she held out.

"Ms. Tyler."

She smiled and his gut flipped. "Please, it's Destiny."

"Destiny. I'm Micah."

"It's a pleasure. I'm so grateful you stopped to get me. And waited an extra three hours."

He grinned, seeing her eyes light at his smile. "Anything for the bride." He picked up her suitcase. "I'm parked close."

"Thank you." She slid into her sleek, dark blue jacket. "I can't wait to see her. It's been nearly a year, and I've never met her fiancé."

His shearling fleece coat felt rustic compared to her New York duds. "They seem happy." He led the way to the parking garage and his truck.

"I know Tracy's very happy." Her heels clicked along beside him. "You grew up with Dade, right?"

Holding open the door to the garage, he let her go through first. Her scent was spicy, Christmassy, like nutmeg and cinnamon. "Yes, ma'am. His family owns the ranch next to mine. Just north of Fort Collins."

She waited for him to step next to her. "Then, this wasn't too far out of your way?"

He put his hand on her lower back and guided her toward his rig. "Not at all. I had to come through Denver to get to Vail."

Destiny shivered and tucked down into her coat. "You sure didn't have to wait three extra hours.

Especially with the snow coming down the way it is. But I'm very glad you did." She grinned at him, her teeth chattering.

"Not a problem." When they were close enough, he started his black super-duty truck with the remote.

"Auto start? Fancy."

He chuckled. "It came with the truck. It's convenient when I'm carrying passengers." *Who aren't dressed for the weather,* he added silently. He opened the passenger door and helped her up, her body surprisingly light. Opening the door to the back seat, he tucked her bag on the floor. As he walked around back past his truck's topper, he glanced inside to make sure all the supplies he'd brought were still settled in the truck bed.

With the snowstorm they were expecting later in the day, he wanted to make sure he had everything they needed to survive. Just in case. By his calculations, they'd be in Vail before the worst of it hit, but they'd have to drive straight through. Damn. If Dade wasn't his best friend, and if Micah hadn't been the best man… Who the hell got married in Vail in the middle of winter?

He glanced out the side of the parking garage. The snow blew across the bright security light. As he slid into his seat, he watched Destiny warm her fingers in front of the heat vent. Long, tapered fingers with short, red-polished nails. Her hair wedged forward, covering her face. He'd just taken off his hat and leaned back between the seats to set it on the back bench when she turned toward him.

Inches separated their faces. He looked into eyes that had seemed gray in the airport, but were a mossy green under the truck's interior light. The moment stretched on as they gazed unsurely at each other. She blinked and pulled back.

He released the breath he'd been holding and put his hands on the steering wheel. Well, hell. Whatever that had been was potent. Shockwaves raced through his cock, setting it to jerk and jitter. This was a little nuts. He didn't know this woman, except for what Tracy had told him. That had included all the usuals; pretty, sweet, fun, easy to get along with. She'd forgotten sexier than sin.

Since college, Destiny had been a high fashion model, living a completely different lifestyle from his. Yet… He glanced at her. There was an intense connection sparking between them.

She watched him. "Tracy said your eyes were blue, but I've never seen irises that color before."

He furrowed his brows. Strange conversation for the first five minutes they'd known each other.

Destiny's gaze ranged over his face. "With your black hair, those blue eyes, and that killer jawline…" She sucked in a breath and let it out with a, "Whew. You could make a fortune modeling."

He was speechless for a moment. Then a bark of laughter boomed out of him. "I'm a cattle rancher, ma'am." He opened his door and stepped out just long enough to take off his coat. Jumping back into the truck, he closed the door and set the coat behind him on the back seat. "No one would want me hawking cough syrup or diapers."

As he shifted into reverse, it was her turn to laugh. "I was thinking more along the lines of men's clothing, but if you're dead set on selling diapers, I can try to make it happen for you."

He glanced at her. The sparkle in her eyes caught him by surprise.

He grinned back. "Thanks, but I'd surely die of culture shock in New York." He shifted into drive and headed out onto the slick roads.

"How about Denver?"

He shrugged. "How about it?"

"I'm moving here next month. I'm opening my own modeling agency."

Braving a glance at her, he quickly shot his eyes back to the traffic exiting the airport. She looked excited. What would it be like to have her this close? A quick hour's drive from his ranch—in good weather. Maybe stranded at the ranch for a few days in the middle of January.

His mind shifted to focus on driving as he pulled onto I-70 heading west toward Vail. Traffic was light this early on a weekday, but the going was slow. Snowplows hulked along, their warning lights flashing, shoving snow off to the side with their huge blades while spewing "Ice Slice" de-icer out their back ends.

When Micah changed lanes to avoid a plow on the left shoulder, his truck bounced over the icy buildup between the lanes. It skidded, the rear end fishtailing.

Destiny braced a hand on the dashboard and gripped the "oh shit" handle above the side door.

"We're fine." He used the voice he calmed his horses with. "It's a bit greasy."

She relaxed back into the seat and dropped her hands in her lap. "Do you think we should pull over for the night? Try again in the morning?"

"No. The snow is gonna come down all night, and it's gonna get a lot heavier toward morning. If we want to make it for the rehearsal this afternoon, we'd better keep going as long as we can."

"Okay."

"Are you hungry? Thirsty? Right behind my seat there's a cooler with water and soda. The box next to it has snacks."

She reached behind him, her head nearly on his shoulder. Her spicy scent snuck up and into his nostrils. His lungs tightened as his belly jittered, spiking desire down into his balls. Temptation caught him, urging him to lean over and nuzzle her hair, the spot where it ended at her neck.

"What would you like?" she asked.

He grunted, the sweetness of her voice throwing

him even further into fantasy.

She sat up and held a water bottle.

"Anything with caffeine, please. And some of that jerky, too." He glanced at her.

She smiled. "I was eyeing that, as well. Not on my regular diet, but it looks delicious. Did you make it?"

"The ranch's cook makes it. It stores well in the line shacks."

"Oh." She set his Coke and her water in the cup holders between their seats. Digging in her purse, she pulled out a small packet of hand wipes, offered him one, which he took, and she used one herself. "I guess I don't even know what a line shack is." She opened the Ziplock bag of jerky and handed him a chunk.

They talked about his ranch for twenty minutes. Her questions were intelligent and insightful.

She pulled out a small chocolate bar and they split it. "A rare treat," she called it. He asked about her work, and she told stories that had them both laughing. When she explained why she was giving up modeling to help aspiring models in the Denver area, he was impressed.

"I'm still in demand, but my interest has shifted as I've grown older."

He shot her a look. She barely looked twenty-five.

"I'll be thirty this year." She smiled at his arched brow. "And it's time for me to share what I've learned."

Tracy had been right. He liked her. Their dialogue

ranged from serious to joking, from light to deep subjects. When he noticed her yawning, he reached back and pulled his coat between their seats. "Use this, if you'd like. Put the seat back and sleep a while."

She placed a hand on his jacket, caressing the sueded skin then the fleecy lining. "Are we almost there?"

"No. I'm taking it slow. It'll be another couple hours or so."

Picking up his coat, she snugged part of it over herself and bunched the rest against the door, laying her head on it. She breathed deeply and sighed.

A rogue fist of possessiveness gripped him. Made him proud to have her use his coat. Made him want to keep her warm and safe.

Well, hell. He'd sure fallen fast.

****

"Aw, shit!"

Micah's shout woke Destiny. She blinked awake, sitting up to look out the window.

The freeway in front of them was covered in a mound of snow, the few cars ahead were being pushed sideways as a wall of white slid down the mountain from their right and buried the vehicles.

Her mouth opened to scream but her lungs froze in shock.

Micah had his foot on the breaks, and the anti-lock system made intermittent grinding noises as it worked to stop the truck without giving up traction. "Shit," he said again as his truck plowed into the heap of snow covering the road.

He immediately shifted into reverse and twisted in his seat, looking back through the truck's rear windows.

The banging sound slammed into her side of the truck first. Outside her window, the view quickly turned into a white wall. The truck slid to the left even as Micah gunned it to move backward.

More banging hit the hood then the roof as their backward movement stopped, replaced by a sideways shove, then a jarring stop. The windshield quickly filled in white.

The whole event had taken only seconds, but it felt like a lifetime. As if she were viewing a horror movie she couldn't turn off.

Looking out Micah's window, she watched as snow piled up until the white barrier surrounded them.

He took her hand. "Are you okay?" His worried gaze comforted her.

"I'm fine. What happened? Where are we?"

"Avalanche." He let go of her hand and pressed on the gas pedal and the truck jerked and shimmied but didn't move. Shifting into drive, he tried again, with the same results. He shut off the engine and turned on the dome light. "We're at Vail Pass. So damn close."

The snow pressing against the windows sent panic flooding from her heart to her chest, numbing her body and choking her breath.

He turned to her and his brow furrowed. "We'll be fine, Destiny."

She could not breathe. Her body shook.

"Destiny." He put his hand on her shoulder. "Look at me."

She tried to focus, but her gaze jumped to the windows. Buried.

His hand cupped her cheek. "We'll be okay." He smiled.

That smile. It had been causing fractures in her composure all night. Now, it served to bring her back from the manic place she'd gone to.

"Breathe, baby. Take a breath for me."

She did and blinked back the fog that had threatened to help her escape into unconsciousness.

"Good. You just keep breathing, now." He took away his hand and opened the storage cubby between their seats. Pulling out a handheld electronic device, he switched it on.

"You're playing video games?"

He laughed and turned the machine toward her. "Avalanche beacon. It'll help the rescuers find us."

He'd come prepared, and she was so relieved.

Micah set the device on the dashboard. "I was buried under an avalanche when I was a teenager." He smiled. "When Dade and me and a couple other guys were heading to Utah to see a rodeo. We were under for about a half hour. There are always people jumping in to help dig out."

Buried. Alive. A fresh stroke of panic took her. "We need to get out." She pressed the button to roll down her window but he took her hand.

"Let me see how far we're under. We may be able to dig out. But if it's more than a few feet, we'll have to wait."

"Why? I can help." The terror in her voice shocked her.

"The snow's too heavy." His thumb caressed her palm. "When the slab is rolling down the hill, it heats up from the friction." He gestured to the windshield. "See how wet it is? It'll freeze again and harden. That'll be when we can try to dig if no one has come around by then." He unfastened his seatbelt. I'm going to get a board and see how far we're under."

"Do we need to make an air hole?" Suddenly her breaths were coming too fast.

"Slow it down, Destiny. We've got plenty to breathe. The snow has air in it. People have survived for days in their cars."

She nodded and paced her breaths.

He climbed into the back seat, his big body heavy with muscle, but limber and bendy.

He opened the back window of the truck and reached into the truck bed. "I ordered the rig with a steel topper. Otherwise, if it was fiberglass or aluminum, this would be crushed."

She appreciated his foresight. Even as she felt an odd sensation. Crushed. They could be crushed. More snow could come down and crush them. The truck's windows started closing in on her. "Oh, God," she cried and pulled his coat up over her head.

His arm came across her front, his head pressing solidly against the top of hers. "Take it easy, baby. I'm here with you. Nothing is going to happen to you."

A shiver rattled through her. "This never happens in New York."

He chuckled. "I'd be acting the same way if I got stuck in the crowds there. Truth be told, I'd rather face an avalanche than a New York sidewalk during rush hour."

A laugh lifted out of her chest. Her shivering stopped. She peeked up over the collar of his jacket.

The lower portion of his body was in the back seat, but his face was right there. They stared for a moment before he tipped his head, she tilted hers, and their lips met.

Firm and warm, his mouth covered hers. A soft kiss, a tentative foreplay. He moved back then, staring at her. "That'll keep me warm." His voice came out husky.

She smiled. "If you did that to distract me, it worked." She no longer felt panic. She felt hot. Dangerously sensual.

He grinned, that handsome smile nearly throwing her back into his arms.

The overhead light went off. Midnight dark.

She gasped.

He leaned forward and something on the dashboard clicked as the light went back on. "In the glove box. There's a flashlight. Take it out and hang onto it."

She knew he was just placating her, giving her something to hold in her hands like a safety blanket. But she did as he asked.

He knelt on the back seat and resumed his leaning through the window into the topper. This time, she was calm enough to admire his bottom. Narrow hips and a scrumptious ass in nice, tight jeans. His thighs were bulky, muscular. Following a naughty urge, she turned on the flashlight and shone it on him. She ran it up his thighs and over his butt. Until she noticed him looking at her.

Heat crept up her neck onto her face and she had to fight the giggle bubbling up from her belly.

"Having fun?" he asked with a grin.

"Sorry." She set down the flashlight and got to her knees facing the back seat. "Can I help?

The cold wafted in from the truck's back end, starting her shivering again.

"Yeah. Could you guide this two-by-four so it doesn't break anything?" He passed her a four-foot length of wood and she eased it into front seat. He had the other end, and he'd put on a pair of work gloves. "Turn the ignition to the left, please."

She did.

He rolled the back window down about a foot, keeping his hand on the snow, shoving back what hadn't fallen into the truck.

"Can we run the motor for a few minutes? Just to get some heat."

He grimaced. "Sorry, the tailpipe is probably plugged with snow."

"Oh." She kind of understood the problem. "Asphyxiation?"

"Uh huh."

He redirected the piece of wood toward the window and gave it a shove. It went through the snow but dumped a pile inside onto the seat.

She covered her mouth with her fingers. Would it flood in on them? Bury them inside the truck?

He shoved and slammed the wood back and forth making a decent size hole, but the slushy snow kept filling it in and dumping piles into the truck. "Huh." He sat back.

"Huh?"

He looked at her. "It's deeper than I thought."

Micah pulled the wood back in and stowed it in the truck bed.

When he'd rolled up the back window, he said, "Okay, turn off the ignition, please." He pulled a couple blankets and a small duffle bag in from the back and closed the window to the topper. "We're going to have to wait for the snow to refreeze."

"Okay." She noticed him shivering and handed his coat to him. She was shivering, too.

"Hang on to that." He sucked in a breath, looking uncertain. "Actually, we should share our body heat."

She blinked a couple times. That was the best idea she'd heard in a long while. "Up here or back there?"

"I'll come up there." He came her way, boots first.

She lifted up as he sat, then eased down onto his lap. This was nice.

"This is nice," he said.

"You read my mind."

He unzipped the duffle and pulled out two stocking caps. "Colorado Tigers or Colorado Avalanche?"

"Oh, jeez, no more avalanche. Tigers, please." She pulled the black and yellow hat on her head. It warmed her ears instantly. He pulled his red cap over his sexy, black hair. She reached up and adjusted his so the logo was front and center.

"Thanks. Just in case we end up on the news, I want to look sharp."

"The news?"

"Free publicity for your business. Start working on your sound bites."

She laughed. "How do you know about those?"

"We do have television reception now, way out in the country."

"Sorry." She snuggled closer, sitting sideways on his lap.

He groaned.

She froze. "Did I hit something…"

His eyes lit with a naughty gleam. "Unless you want to cause a problem for me, you'll sit still."

Biting her lip, she grinned. "Hmm. And if I don't?" That was so wicked.

He stopped and looked at her. "You've got something in mind, don't you."

"In fear for your chastity?" Oh, jeez, what had gotten into her?

"Baby, we may only have a half hour before Search and Rescue arrives, but I'm willing to compromise my chastity."

A shiver ran through her. Partially the cold, mainly her desire.

He opened a blanket and spread it over their legs then resettled his coat over her and around him.

She turned on her flashlight. "Should we save the truck battery?"

He turned off the dome light. "Battery's good, but the light was too bright."

"Cozy," she murmured, setting the flashlight on the driver's seat. Beneath her hip, she felt a rise behind his fly. She wiggled. "I'm getting warmer. You?"

He laid his hand on her thigh. The coolness of his skin surprised her. She set her hand on top of his and rubbed his palm over her pant leg. "You're cold."

His other hand snuck under the back of her coat and touched her through her sweater. It was chilly, too. "You're heating me up. Fast."

Destiny skimmed her hand over his chest. Through his shirt she felt him, strong and hot, bunched muscles. She unbuttoned until his dark chest hair sprung from between the fabric. "I love a man with chest hair."

"Don't all male models wax?"

She shook her head. "No. I'd leave you just the way you are." She looked into his eyes. "Actually, you're much more appealing as a cowboy than a model. I rescind my offer of work."

"Can't say I'm surprised. I'm cut rough."

Tingling started in her breasts and echoed in her core. "How rough?"

"As rough as you like it, baby." His expression echoed devilish intent.

His hands, running up and down her thigh and over her back, finally warmed.

Destiny bracketed his face with her palms. "Micah, I want to tell you. This is the wildest thing I've ever done." She'd heard so many stories about him from her best friend, Tracy, she'd felt she almost knew him intimately before she'd walked up to him in the airport. It was probably why Tracy had asked Micah to pick her up. A little bit of matchmaking going on.

She glanced around her. "Trapped under tons of snow with a virtual stranger. But it feels so right." He felt so right.

"Mm hm. I'm getting the same impression." He met her gaze. "Now, just exactly what is this wild thing you're planning?"

Smiling, she pressed her lips to his. "If you're willing, I'm going to impinge on your chastity—"

He moved then, fast as a panther. His hand cupped the back of her head and he kissed her, devouring her, his tongue taking and testing, sucking hers into his mouth and nibbling on her as if she were his last meal. Against her lips, he growled, "Baby, I'm willing."

Her core flooded with heat, her thighs clenched tightly together, she wiggled, rubbing her pussy against her clothing, the friction making her dizzy.

His mouth slanted over hers again, teasing, tongue against tongue. Sliding his hand under her shirt, he caressed her back before unfastening her bra. With both hands, he took her breasts in his large palms and circled, squeezed lightly. "You're amazing."

When her nipples tightened to intense points, the race of lust washed to her core, moistening her cunt and making her hips buck.

"So responsive," he murmured, and lifted her shirt.

Lacing her fingers in his silky hair, she guided him to her breast.

He took nearly one whole breast into his mouth, sucking, swirling his tongue around and around until he pinpointed her nipple. Sucking greedily, he made her manic with the tugs that whirled through her body, ending at her slit.

He treated her other breast to the same sexy foreplay and nibbled on her beaded nipple until her clit pulsed with its own beat.

"Micah, you are so, so good."

He hummed against her breast, sucking her nipple in further.

Her ass went from wiggling in need to circling in desperation. His hard cock under her hips taunted her with its nearness.

Moving his hand to her belly, he stroked her flesh. The calluses on his palm rough but completely sexy against her pampered skin. In seconds, he'd unfastened her pants and had his fingers deep inside.

Destiny leaned back slightly, and tipped her hips up in encouragement.

Lifting his head from her breast, he looked into her eyes. The shadows cast by the flashlight's beam made him look like pure sin.

"Take me, Micah," she begged.

His fingers dipped lower and cupped her bare pussy. For long moments he skimmed his hand over her, just feeling. His eyes narrowed, darkened, as he explored. "You're wet and slick. I want to taste you. Eat you for hours. Make you come for me until you pass out."

His words hit her like a wave and carried her away on a riptide. "Yes, please."

When his finger touched her clit, he circled it, slow and steady.

She felt his gaze on her as he brought her up toward heaven again. Then his mouth fastened on her breast and her body jerked. Waves of pleasure overtook her and with an unexpected fierceness, she popped over the top, rolling and ebbing, flowing and shuddering. Her climax took her deep, where no sound could reach, then sent her floating back toward the surface, her breaths coming like the waves on the sand, her skin alternately hot then cool.

His arms came around her and she opened her eyes. "Micah, that was incredible."

His eyes moved, studying her face. "You're beautiful, but when you come, you're irresistibly gorgeous."

She smiled and stroked his cheek. "There it is."

"What?"

"The sound bite. For when we're interviewed."

He laughed again, the sound filling the small space and making her ridiculously happy.

He took her lower lip between his teeth and tickled her flesh with his tongue. He let her loose and whispered against her mouth, "What's your sound bite gonna be?"

She nipped his bottom lip just as he'd done to her.

She looked into his eyes and her core gave a jitter. "I made love to this sexy cowboy and made him come in ten minutes."

He smiled and slowly shook his head. "Can't be done. I've got at least an hour's worth of stamina in me."

She laughed. "You can prove that to me later…" Her smile faded. Would there be a later?

"Baby." His eyes went dark and heavy lidded. "I'll prove it to you. A dozen times after we get out of this truck." He cocked his head as if listening outside. Silence. "Right now, I want you to prove *your* claim."

Every inhibition deserted her. She wanted him. "Condom?"

"Wallet." He reached and found it.

She unbuckled him, unsnapped, unzipped, and tugged his jeans and boxers down.

He was huge. Long and wide, leaning to the right, his mushroom-shaped head already beading with lubrication. "This proves that old saying wrong." She grinned, shooting a wicked glance at him. "What do they say about men with big trucks having small *parts*?"

His lips quirked. "It's not the size of the truck, but how you use it." The condom he handed her was extra-large.

She laughed, remembering the commercial. "You've been blessed with a big truck, and a big…" She glanced sideways at him. "Ego."

He chuckled until her hand gripped his pulsing cock. He sucked in a breath and his eyes closed as a groan rumbled from his chest.

Hard and searing against her skin, she stroked his shaft a few times before rolling on the condom.

He got busy, struggling to work her pants down her thighs. When they caught at her knees, she said, "Good enough. I don't have time to take my boots off. They're laced." She'd only given herself ten minutes to prove her skills, and the clock was ticking. "Spread your legs a little."

He obeyed, leaned back, stacked his hands behind his head, and grinned. "It's your show, Destiny."

She smiled. "Hold on, cowboy. It's gonna be a wild one."

His eyes shut for a second. "Fuck," he muttered under his breath.

Destiny's legs were pinned together at the knees with her clothing. She eased her legs between his and planted her boots on the floor. Straightening her legs, she leaned over the dashboard. She watched him appreciate her round ass and a sneak peak of pussy. The cool air shimmied over her skin, but she was heated from the inside by waves of pure desire.

"Nice." He said it like a starving man.

Easing back, she reached for him.

"I like the boots." He stared at her bottom, his teeth gritted, his breath coming faster.

"We'll have lots of fun with them later. When you

prove your stamina."

He groaned and his cock jumped.

With his big shaft in her palm, she eased herself back. Her soaking pussy easily lubricated the condom.

The heat of his cock burned into her as she slowly took him in, giving her body a second to adjust.

"So. Fucking. Tight." His words rolled out like rocks in a grinder.

The intensity of him filling her to capacity ravaged through her, centering in her nipples and tingling at her clit.

Grabbing the handle above the door with one hand, and the steering wheel with the other, she started her ride. With her legs pressed together, the fit was extremely tight. To enhance the effect—and stay within her ten-minute goal—she clenched her pussy, squeezing her core around him.

"Too much," he moaned.

It was. She was feeling the overload herself. A swirling pleasure stole up her spine, whirling in her brain. Was she going to come before he did?

"You look hot, baby. Sexy. Riding my cock." His hands cupped her ass cheeks.

She had to concentrate, but a whining moan came from her throat.

"Yeah, you're gonna come with me. Your sweet pussy is gonna squeeze me so tight it'll get you off like a rocket."

His naughty words and thick shaft raised her temperature until she couldn't keep her eyes open.

He grabbed her hips and guided her movements. Faster and rougher, her cowboy met her downward slides with an upward pump, slamming his shaft into her, his pelvis against her ass and thighs, her cunt lips against his thick, wiry hairs.

"Feels incredible!" Her brain whizzed into semi-consciousness as an orgasm surprised her.

"Yeah, baby. I'm gonna come inside you." His growled words accompanied his body tensing, his fingers digging into her hips, his breath chugging like a freight train.

She let herself spin wildly through a fast, hot climax, her arms shook, her legs quivered, her slit juiced and tightened with each thrust.

Floating back to reality, she registered his satisfied moans.

His hands on her hips slowed her, steadied her ride, then came to a jerking halt. "You rode me, Destiny. No doubt. You found my weakness."

Circling her hips while clenching her slit, she leaned back against him. "Uh uh. You are wickedly powerful." She cupped his cheek and turned her face to kiss his jaw. "I don't know if you noticed or not, but you gave me The Big O without even touching my happy spot."

He laughed, his belly shaking against her back. "Happy spot." He wrapped his arms around her stomach and squeezed. "Just imagine what I'll be able to do with a real bed and a couple hours to explore the happiest place on your body."

A thrill of excitement rattled through her.

"Cold?" He kissed her cheek and nuzzled her hair.

"No. Just…excited for later." When they could spend time getting to know each other's bodies, and each other's hearts.

He took a breath and waited a few seconds. "When we get out of here, get the truck dug out and running, they'll send us back to Copper Mountain until they get the road cleared."

"Enough time for us to get a room?"

"Mm hm. Exactly what I was thinking." His hands ranged over her flesh, her thighs, her belly, her stomach. "Plenty of time to grab some sleep and a shower."

"And?"

"And prove my stamina." His cock jerked inside her.

"I'd like that."

He took a deep breath again.

She recognized it as his hesitation before asking something important.

"How long are you in Colorado? After the wedding, I mean?"

Smiling, she turned to look into his eyes. He had such a piercing gaze. "Eleven days. I'm hoping to beg a ride back to Denver from you." She batted her eyes at him. "I need to check out the apartment I rented sight-unseen, and the storefront that's being renovated for me."

"Well, hell, Destiny, you know you have a ride with me any time." He pumped his hips to emphasize the type of ride he meant. "And if you have a few extra days…"

"Mm hm?" She smiled and traced his lips with her thumb.

He nipped at her, and licked the tip of her thumb.

She moaned and took back her hand. She needed to pull herself out of this afterglow before they were rescued, or she'd be grinning like a naughty kitty.

"Come up to my ranch with me."

Her brow furrowed. How lucky was she to find a man like this?

His gaze dropped. "You can think about it if—"

"No." She set her palms on his cheeks and waited until he looked at her again. "I don't have to think about it. I'd love to spend time with you."

He tunneled his hands into her hair and kissed her.

Thumping sounded on the roof.

Destiny jerked back and her eyes opened wide. Was the roof caving in under the snow?

"It's just Search and Rescue probing the snow."

The thumping came in two three-tap bursts.

Micah reached over and tooted the horn twice. "We'll be out in a few minutes."

The distant sound of crunching snow filtered into

the truck.

They tossed off the blanket and coat and helped each other dress. When they were decent, Micah shone the flashlight beam on the side window. It was covered with frost, and so was the right half of the windshield. "Look at that. And you worried about keeping warm."

She scratched a nail down the window, sending flakes of frost flying. "I guess I don't know my own temperature." She grinned at him.

"Baby, you're hot. And you heat me up like a furnace. Hell, I'm surprised the snow didn't melt from around the truck with the body heat we gave off."

"Well, hell, cowboy," she echoed his earlier comment. "Wait 'till we get to our hotel room." She looked at him from under her lashes. "We may have to turn on the air conditioner."

~~~~
~~~~

Breakfast in Bed

Nate McMurphy woke as the click of his front door closing told him Misti Garnett was sneaking out. Again. He reached across her empty pillow and turned the digital clock toward him. Two fourteen AM. "Goddamn." Tossing off the sheet, he walked naked to the side window.

The tail lights of her '67 Mustang wound out of his driveway, turned onto the ranch's main road that headed past the big house, and disappeared over the ridge. She'd take a right on the county road and head home to her dad's ranch eight miles away.

He rubbed one eye with his palm as he walked back into his bedroom and looked out the window. The river running past his house reflected the half-moon back to him. Half was all he got from Misti, too. Half a night. She'd come home with him a couple dozen times. She never stayed, though, even when he'd asked her. Her excuses ranged from "early classes tomorrow" to "Dad'll worry."

Was it this place? Yeah, it was a bachelor pad. He'd only been ranch foreman for a year, and hadn't had a chance to fix it up much.

He turned and looked at the bed. A double-size mattress and box spring sitting on a metal frame. One corner dipped lower, held up by a cinder block. His old white sheets, clean but scratchy, and a Texas

A&M blanket he'd gotten from the Dollar Store in town lay half on the floor.

"Hell. No wonder she won't stay."

Heading out to the dining room, he fired up his computer. He'd take the ranch's enclosed truck into Abilene today and see if he could round up some better furniture. It would cost him part of the money he'd saved to buy his own ranch, but he'd tried everything to get Misti to spend the night. Maybe a nice king-size bed would keep her here. He wanted her with him.

She was beautiful, sure, but she sparked with life. Everyone was her friend. She did more than her share for the church and community projects. She'd talk to him for hours, telling him about her dreams of becoming a teacher so she could find a job and stay close to home. She'd listen to him for hours, too, talk about the ranch he'd have some day.

Whenever she smiled at him, everything inside stopped for a second.

He ran his fingers though his wavy, blonde hair. He kept it a little long, just the way she liked it. "Nate, buddy," he told himself as he searched for the furniture store online. "You're in deep."

****

Four days later, Nate opened the drivers' door on Misti's car and offered a hand to help her out.

She looked at him strangely. "What's this about?" They'd met for dinner, gone dancing, and she'd followed him home from the bar after. As usual. She never let him pick her up. She needed her getaway car for her pre-dawn escape.

"Bein' a gentleman, ma'am." He grinned, putting a dose of wicked into his eyes. Inside, his stomach jittered. Would she like it? He'd gone a ways overboard, but once the lady at the store had his story, she'd sold him a truck full.

Wrapping his arm around her shoulder, he led her up the porch steps to the door. The chill December wind blew her long, blonde hair across his face. The scent of peaches called his cock to attention and his balls drew tight. He opened the door and let her step into the dark living room first.

Misti reached over and flipped the switch. Instead of the bare light bulb on the ceiling, two brand-new table lamps came on. "Oh." She tugged off her cowgirl boots and walked into the room. Touching the new coffee table, she glanced at him, an amazed look in her eyes. "You decorated?"

Yanking off his Resistol, he cussed himself for feeling like a sissy. Cowboys. Don't. Decorate. "I decided it was time to make the place home. I won't have money to buy my own land for a few more years, so…" So, yeah, okay, he'd decorated.

She looked at him, her blue eyes warm and gentle. Just like her. "I like it." Her gaze moved behind him. "Curtains, too?"

Clasping his hat brim, he turned it in his hands a

couple times before stopping himself and hanging it on the coat tree. "Curtains, too." The woman at the store had told him his roll-down shades weren't 'real' window covering. "Can I take your coat?"

It took a few seconds of her staring at him before she unbuttoned her fleece-lined denim jacket and handed it to him. He hung it next to his hat, and slipped out of his jean jacket, hanging it close to hers. Kind of homey, that coat tree holding their things. Better than throwing their coats on the couch on the way into the bedroom, like they used to.

He took her hand and led her to the back of the house. Into his bedroom. He snapped on the light and stepped aside, watching her face.

She sucked in a quick breath and a smile followed. "It's gorgeous." She walked in and ran her fingers along the dark oak dresser, then over the mission-style footboard that matched the headboard. She plopped down on top of the golden bedspread and bent forward, her head between her knees. "You bought a dust ruffle?"

He huffed out a breath. Sissy. "The store lady—"

"I love it, Nate." She sat up and bounced on the bed a couple times. "It's so cozy here."

Cozy enough that she'd stay the night? He crossed to her and pulled her up into his arms. "Darlin'." He rubbed his hard, hot cock against her mound. "Let's break it in."

She laughed and tugged his shirt off over his

head, threw it aside, and went right for his jeans. The first time was always wild, but tonight, she was feral. Their clothes ended up in a pile next to one of his new nightstands.

"How do you want it, cowboy?" Her breath panted from her lips, her eyelids drooped, sexy and hungry.

Every drop of blood from his brain rushed to his staff. His ass tightened and released. He needed to be pumping his cock into her soft, hot slit. Smelling her musk, he cupped a hand over her nearly-bare pussy. What creative shape had she gotten waxed into her blonde curlies this week? He'd get a close-up view a little later. Right now, he had to get that first rush of sliding his shaft all the way inside her tight opening. Juices dripped from her swollen lips as his fingers stroked, slowly at first, then faster, carrying her natural lubricant up to her hard little clit.

Each pass of his fingers made her shudder and gasp, until she had no muscle left to stand. He turned her to face the bed, lifted her, and set her face down on his new comforter.

She stretched and writhed on the fabric, sending his balls contracting and his lower back spasming. Fuck. If he didn't get control, it'd be over with one thrust. He grabbed a condom and rolled it on, then crawled onto the bed, up on all fours over her.

"Nathan. Take me." It drove him insane when she called him 'Nathan.' It meant she was close. Right on the edge. The way her hair spread across his bed brought a yearning inside him. This was where she belonged. Her face in profile so beautiful, glimpses of her full breasts teased him as she wiggled and arched her back.

Grasping her wrists, he tugged them up over her head and pressed his body full-length on top of hers, his shaft settling in the sweet crack between her ass cheeks. She gasped for breath under his weight, but he knew she liked it. Liked being restrained. Beneath him, she was soft and warm, smelling sweet and sexy, making his skin tingle where they touched.

With his knees, he spread her legs wide open for him. Under his hips, her ass pushed up as she arched her back. "Now, Nathan. Please." Her voice came out barely a whisper.

Taking both her wrists in one hand, he slid his other hand slowly down her arm, knowing she liked the scratch of his calluses. He brushed his fingers over her armpit, feeling her body quiver, then touched lower, over her side. He found her breast and palmed it, firm and satin-soft, he would spent hours kissing and sucking and nibbling tonight. And hopefully tomorrow morning, too.

When he pinched her nipple between his splayed fingers, she cried out and her body jerked. Her hips moved to an animal rhythm, humping into his cock, nearly setting him off. He needed her. He reared back with his hips and settled the tip of his erection at her slit. Her hot, slick opening burned the head of his pulsing shaft. Then he entered her, his length stretching her as he greedily took her and generously gave her what she craved.

She moaned, long and low, tipping her head back.

He suckled her neck, careful not to bruise. His cock moved into her, then out in mindless, primitive plunges. His body shook, the ache in his lower back spread to his balls. They tightened, ready to shoot his cum into her, needing to mark her as his own.

Releasing her wrists, he slid his hand between the satin comforter and her stomach, then lower, finding her clit hiding in her full, wet pussy lips. His finger touched her, rubbed twice, and she came. She screamed his name, her body shuddering and stiffening, her core clenching around him, forcing him to follow her.

His release was monumental, drowning him as waves of pleasure rolled through him. His hips strained to go deeper, as far inside her as he could get. His mind sank to the bottom of a dark pool, never wanting this to end, wanting her with him every time he felt this release.

When he collapsed beside her, he pulled her close. Her breath panted, her body after-shocking with shudders and sighs.

His last thought before drifting off was selfish. How could he keep her here—permanently?

Nate woke with the first rays of the rising sun on

his face, streaming through the curtains he'd left open last night so they could look at the river as they made love. Seven times last night. An all-time record for them. He smiled. Who was counting. He rolled over. Her side of the bed was empty. "Shit." All the time he'd spent picking out things he thought she'd like—and that he could live with. He made this place a home for them, and she… Did he smell coffee?

He sat up and breathed deeply. Coffee and bacon? He belly-flopped across the bed and looked over the edge. There were his clothes—and hers—still in a pile. The grin that broke across his face was the silent cry of 'yee-haw!' that burst through his brain. She'd stayed.

Her quiet laugh came from the doorway. "What are you doing?"

He glanced up.

She padded into the room looking messy and sexy in one of his old t-shirts, carrying the tray he'd bought at the home store. She set it down on the nightstand next to him. Coffee, bacon and eggs, and cut-up fruit.

A crazy emotion bubbled up. Home. This felt like home. Something he'd been missing in his life. It'd almost seemed out of reach.

He grabbed her around the waist and pulled her into bed with him.

She squealed as she landed in his lap, and pushed her hair out of her face. Leaning forward, she kissed him, tasting like coffee with sugar.

He had to know, even if it was obvious. "Why'd you stay, Misti?"

Her eyes grew shiny and she blinked a few times. "It's silly."

"Tell me." He kissed her, quick and soft.

She sighed, snuggling into him. "When we made love that last time…" She shivered a little and a naughty glint sparkled in her eyes. "After we took a shower, you handed me that brand new pink toothbrush."

He nodded. He'd seen it in the drugstore in Abilene when he'd swung in to stock up on condoms, and knew she'd like it. He waited for her to continue, but she didn't. He frowned. "That's it? A two-dollar toothbrush?"

She giggled. "Everything else you did to the place is great. Really nice. But when you handed me that toothbrush…" She shrugged. "I knew you were serious."

Well, son of a gun. That was all it took? "I am serious, darlin'. I want you here." He ran to the edge and took the plunge. "Move in with me."

Her eyes widened. "Wow. I didn't realize how serious you were." She sat up and stared out at the river.

Shit. Had he gone too far? Would she run now?

Swinging around, she looked at him with worried eyes. "Okay."

His heart triple-beat. She'd said yes. But

something wasn't right.

"One thing, though," she said.

Uh oh. "What?"

She dropped back on the bed and looked up at him. "Will you make *me* breakfast in bed once in a while?"

He leaned down and kissed her, and between each kiss said, "Every. Single. Morning." A promise he would keep for the rest of his life.

~ ~ ~ ~

Hard Headed Cowboy

Cade Carter flashed his association card. The half-sleeping security guard waved him through the back entrance of the temporary arena. The second day of the two-day rodeo near Rapid City, South Dakota, and Cade was in the top three. He was the only contestant there so far, but he'd come early to meet a man who might rightly change the outcome of his bull riding career.

Making a pit stop in the men's room, he combed his short black hair and resettled his black cowboy hat. Re-tucking his shirttails, he double-checked to make sure his jeans were zipped and buttoned, and his championship belt buckle shone.

He walked past the chutes taking a quick look at the bulls. One of these ugly bastards would try to kill him today. And Cade would have eight seconds to convince him otherwise.

Just outside the restricted area was a roped off section of ground for the media and sponsors. A few people stood around talking as he entered. His gaze caught on an eye-popper. A little redhead in a tank top and jeans who, from the back, snared his interest.

She turned toward him, her shoulder-length hair flying, catching the light. A pretty face, nice C cups, and a big sexy smile for him. She walked toward him, her hips swaying, her cowgirl boots kicking up dust.

He tucked his thumbs in his belt. He'd had buckle bunnies chasing him *after* the rodeo, but not many *before*. This one was a definite "yes, ma'am."

"Cade? Cade Carter?" Her green eyes locked with his blue ones. She knew her rodeo cowboys, alright.

"Yes, ma'am, that's me." She was a sight prettier up close and his cock jerked in welcome.

Reaching out a hand, she said, "I'm Terri Josephs from HeadStar Equipment. It's so nice to meet you."

Aw, crap. This was the man…woman…he was meeting. He shook her hand, surprised at the force behind the grip. "It's a pleasure." He tipped his hat and cooled his lust.

She made a face. "You were expecting a man, weren't you."

At first he shook his head, then he smiled and nodded. "I've never seen a female sponsor's rep. 'Cept in the barrel racing and such." Damn, he was talking like a hick. His first meeting with a sponsor and he was blowing it.

"We based our preliminary equipment rollout on the timed events. Men's and women's. But we've branched out and that's why I'm here to see you." Her eyes sparkled with excitement and her smile grew even brighter. She was a sparkplug.

"Would you like to…" they both said in unison.

She laughed.

"Should we find a place to sit and talk?" He nodded to the empty arena.

They strolled through the dry summer heat into the seating area. "There's a good spot." He pointed behind her. A portion of the bleachers were in the shade.

She hefted her big purse onto her shoulder and climbed ahead of him, up a few steps to a relatively cool spot on the aluminum bench. He kept his eyes off her ass. Mostly.

"I snuck in and took a peek at the bulls earlier." She bit her lower lip. "Does it make you nervous, knowing you'll be riding in a few hours?"

Glancing behind the chutes, Cade saw the pens where the broncs stood with their buddy horses. Waiting patiently for their big moment. Just like he was doing. "It's hard to explain." He met her stare. "It's a mean kind of excited."

She gave a low whistle and dug in her purse. "That's an amazing tag line." Pulling out a pad of paper and a pencil, she wrote.

"Tag line?"

Terri took out a fancy black leather folder with the company's logo on the front and she opened it to the first page. His picture was tucked into a plastic sleeve. "Imagine." Her voice came out whispery and sexy. "Our logo here, and your tagline here." She pointed across his knees. "A national campaign."

This was getting more interesting by the minute.

She flipped the page to a picture of black chaps embossed with his name in red leather. Talking a mile a minute about how they would promote him and all the benefits he'd receive, she caught him up in her excitement. The next page showed a vest, the same black and red.

"I like it." Liked her, too. Smart, sexy, and with the focus of a high beam.

She smiled at him, her eyes lit with pleasure.

"Helmets," she flipped the page quickly.

"Whoa, whoa, whoa." He flipped it back. "Helmets? You'd expect me to wear a helmet?"

She looked at him, seeming startled, and blinked a few times. "Everyone's wearing helmets now."

He shook his head. "Mostly cowboys with head injuries."

"It's part of the line we're introducing, so it would be imperative that you start wearing a helmet if you're sponsored by us."

He let out a breath. This he did not want to do. Not a pride thing, just something his dad and grandpa taught him. Real cowboys wore a hat.

"Cade…" Terri touched his arm and their gazes locked. Through his long-sleeved shirt, her hand felt hot. Her touch started a rattle of awareness in his gut. She quickly pulled back her hand and sucked in a breath. Had she felt it, too?

After a moment, she glanced down at her presentation. "Is the helmet a deal breaker?" She looked near to tears.

He liked how every emotion showed on her

face—magnified ten times.

"I don't know." He'd have to think about it. Talk to his dad and grandpa, and his partners, see what they thought.

"Well, let's not worry about that right now." She flipped the page. "Here's the contract." A thick packet of papers was snugged in the back pocket. "Would you like to go over it together, or would you prefer to read it yourself?"

Tapping sounded over the speakers. "Will the contestants please check in," a voice crackled. "All contestants, we're ready for you to check in."

She looked at him with such innocent expectation, he had to give her more of his time. Hell, he'd like to spend a whole lot of his time with her. She was a little high-strung, but he liked his women edgy.

He shifted, pressing his thigh against hers. The flash of desire returned. "Can I take you out for a late supper after the rodeo?"

She smiled, shyly. "I'd like that, but it should be my treat, since it's business."

"Let's call it a date, and we'll handle the business tomorrow morning."

Her eyes went wide, and her mouth formed into a little "O." Bright pink colored her cheeks. "Okay." She took a shaky breath and closed the folder. "Should I hang on to this?"

"Yes. Please." They stood and he took her elbow.

Her arm jittered and he looked into her eyes. Her

pupils expanded, and her lids drooped.

He felt it, too, like heat flowing through his veins. As if on cue, they stepped closer. This was too public. Too risky.

Why didn't he care? He pressed his lips to hers, just a quick kiss to satisfy their curiosity.

It didn't work that way. As if the bleachers were electrified, his body reacted to her soft lips, her spicy perfume, her quiet sigh. His belly clenched as blood flowed lower, down into his staff. Pulling away from her, he watched her face.

Desire, as hot and immediate as his own, blazed in her beautiful eyes and her breath came shallow.

Cade ran his hand up her bare arm. "Wait for me in the same place, inside the media area after the event ends."

"You just be careful out there." Her face showed concern. "You're valuable to us."

He grinned. "I'll wave to you from the bull."

Her laughter bubbled out, and her longing glowed in her eyes. "I'm looking forward to dinner."

"Yes, ma'am. Me, too."

****

The buzzer sounded. He'd ridden the full eight seconds. Cade jumped off Barbequed, landing solid on his feet. But the bull wasn't done with him. The rank bastard swung around, snorting at him, eyeing him with rage.

Everything warped into slow motion.

Cade turned to run for the rails, but a bullfighter tripped him up and he landed flat on his face. "Shit." A second later, a burning pressure hit his right shoulder, shoving him down into the loose dirt. "Fuck."

Men's voices yelled around him, taunting the bull to get him away from Cade. The audience cried out then silenced. The stomp of hooves grew quieter as Barbequed ran off, back into the chutes.

Someone grasped his left shoulder, asking if he was okay.

When he tried to move his right arm, nothing happened for a second, then screaming pain raced through his entire right side.

He let the bullfighter help him up. The agony in his shoulder nearly blacked him out. He took a second to breathe and get his feet under him, then gritted his teeth into a semblance of a smile and waved to the crowd.

A cheer went up and he took a couple tentative steps, then a few more until he made it inside the gate. His partners, Rowdy and Jim, flanked him and silently walked him back to the first aid room.

"Lucky they got him off you when they did," Rowdy said as Cade sat on the table and started unbuttoning his shirt.

"Doesn't feel lucky." His voice sounded gravely as the pain nearly choked him.

"Don't bother with your buttons," the medic told

him. "It's ripped anyway." He cut away the fabric.

"What's the damage, doc?" Jim crossed his arms over his chest.

Cade risked a glance at his shoulder. Things weren't aligned right anymore.

"I'm not going to lie, Cade. It's bad. You need to get to the ER. Right now."

Rowdy stepped closer. "I'll drive him. Jim, you stay and collect our prize money."

Was this the end of his career? Cade wanted to yell. Needed to kick something. Throw something. When he stood, the room swayed and his stomach rolled.

Rowdy and Jim walked with him through the staging area. He glanced toward the media corner, but didn't see Terri. Hell, after seeing him getting stomped into the dirt she'd probably thrown out that fancy leather binder along with his contract.

When they stepped out the contestant door, she was there.

"Cade." Her expressive face showed her worry. "Can I do anything?"

"We're taking him to Rapid City, to the hospital." Jim handed Rowdy the keys to his truck. The three of them had ridden up here together from their last rodeo in Kansas. "Well, Rowdy is, anyway."

"I'm so sorry." She walked with them to the truck.

Cade heard what she *wasn't* saying—*sorry we can't offer you a contract, now.* "Don't be." He opened the truck door. "Once I'm back on the circuit…" Easing onto the seat, he gave her one last look. "There'll be other sponsors coming along." Jim shut the door as she started talking, and Rowdy started the truck.

She gestured for him to roll down his window but he just tipped his hat. Terri and Jim stood there watching him leave. Damn. This had started out the best day of his life. He groaned and held his elbow as the truck bounced over a rut.

And it ended up the worst.

The next morning Cade came out of unconsciousness into a fog but feeling no pain. The surgery had gone well. It was a dislocation and a break. Easy to fix, easier to mend. He'd be back on the circuit in a month or two. Thank God.

They wheeled him into his room where Jim and Rowdy sat playing poker.

"You lived," Jim observed, shuffling the deck.

"Feeling pretty good, too." He used the buttons to raise the head of the bed. "When do we leave?"

The guys looked at each other. "*We're* leaving in an hour for Ottawa. *You're* leaving tomorrow for home."

Ottawa was a big rodeo. He couldn't ask them to pass it up just so he didn't have to ride the Greyhound all the way to Oklahoma. He didn't have the money to fly.

"Yeah, no problem. I'll grab the bus." Would there

be enough painkillers for him to make that trip?

The guys just grinned at him.

"What's funny?"

They went back to playing cards.

"Things'll work out for you." Jim laid down his cards. "Three queens."

Rowdy winked at Cade. "Fourth queen is on her way."

His partners laughed at their inside joke.

Cade was too tired to deal with their bullshit. He let the leftover anesthesia and pain meds take him under.

When he woke to a tapping on his door, the room was empty. "Come."

A redheaded sparkplug stuck her head in the door. "Are you decent?"

His mouth dropped open. He didn't think he'd see her again.

****

Terri's heart sped when she saw him lying in that bed. His shoulder and arm wrapped in bandages, but his chest bare. The mixed emotions of sympathy and desire raced through her. Dark swirls of hair covered his chest. A very well muscled chest, and biceps, and abs. His black hair looked deliciously messed. She ached to comb her fingers through it.

He hadn't moved. Hadn't spoken. Just lay there with his mouth hanging open, his blue eyes unfocused. Maybe the drugs…

"I'm Terri Josephs? From HeadStar Equipment?"

He laughed, a hoarse sound. "I remember you." His gaze dropped to her breasts then shot back up to her eyes. "We were gonna have dinner, weren't we?" He pressed a button and the top half of his bed rose.

She came in and closed the door. "Someone stood me up." She smiled.

He stayed silent for a few seconds. "I'm wondering what you're doing here."

Walking into the room, her stomach jittered nervously. Would he accept her offer? She had overstepped a bit. *Okay, a lot.*

"I talked with Jim and Rowdy while you were in surgery this morning."

He looked surprised, but didn't say anything.

"They were going to give up their next few rodeos to drive you home. I told them I'd take you." She found herself biting her lip, and released it.

He stared. Unmoving.

"I hope that's okay." She swallowed and forged ahead. "When I told the owner of the company what had happened to you, he asked me to assure you we're still interested in sponsoring you, provided you…" She trailed off and gestured to his shoulder.

"I'll ride again. You can count on it."

She loved his conviction. His pride. "The boss okayed me to trade in my rental car for a bigger vehicle, and drive you to Oklahoma." She smiled, but it felt forced. Would his pride allow him to just accept her taking over his life?

"I..." He shook his head, looking baffled. "Why would you do that for me?" His eyes held wonder, astonishment, and maybe a bit of lust, too.

Five months ago, when she'd heard rumors of adding bull riders to the company's sponsorship stable, she'd done research on dozens of rising stars. Cade was not only a damn good bull rider, he was an excellent role model. He'd given talks at schools about focusing on the future and staying away from drugs and gangs. He'd taken part in fundraisers for animal shelters and food shelves in the towns where he'd rodeoed. And he'd set his widowed mother up with a condo in Oklahoma City while he lived in a small apartment. The quote he'd given the local paper was, "She gave me everything I needed when I was a kid. I owe her. But mainly, I love her."

The memory of her tears when she'd read those three sentences brought a fresh burning to the corners of her eyes.

She turned away. Cade had been "her" cowboy, and after her presentation, her boss had agreed he'd be the first bull rider offered the company's sponsorship.

"There's a catch." She set her purse on the chair and took her time walking around to the left side of his bed. "I have to make a couple stops on the way. A couple meetings with clients whom we sponsor. Who would probably love to meet you."

His eyes narrowed. "You're using me as a

marketing tool?"

"No." She waved her hands to erase what she'd just said. "Not at all." A slice of panic wedged under her heart. She was making a mess of this. "If you don't want to meet them, you can stay in the hotel room."

He blinked and a wicked smile curved one corner of his lips. "Hotel room, huh?"

Visions of them together on the bed flashed through her mind. Heat crept up her neck and she stared at the mattress, circling her fingertip on the sheet. "Boss says I can't pay for your hotel room. You have to pay for that yourself." She glanced at him then went back to her circles. "But I thought we could share. You know, save on expenses." Oh, Lord, she sounded like a tramp. "I mean, we can get two beds—"

Grabbing her hand, he tugged her down until she sat on the bed next to his hip. "Terri, sweetheart, nothing has ever sounded as good to me as sharing a room with you." He pulled her close and wrapped his hand around the nape of her neck. His lips met hers, softly for a second, then his tongue traced her bottom lip.

She opened for him, letting his tongue slide into her mouth, touching hers, then playing with it, exploring her mouth. She reciprocated. Lapping his tongue, tickling the bridge of his mouth. Chills traced down her spine and rippled through her body.

Minutes later, both of them breathing heavily, she backed away from him. "You need your rest."

"No." He pulled her down for another wild kiss. He bit her lip gently, the spot she always worried with her teeth, then he licked it and groaned. Or was that her groaning? Her body shimmered with desire, her nipples puckered and between her legs, her core heated and tingled.

She pulled away and stood, panting and shivering with need. If he kept it up, she'd be riding him right here on the hospital bed. Grabbing for a distraction, she picked up the deck of cards off his bedside table. "Let's play poker."

"Only if it's strip poker."

She smiled and fluffed the top sheet that covered his lower body. "What are you wearing under there? Pajama bottoms? I'd win for sure." When the sheet settled over him, she was staring at a huge tent erected over his hips. "Oh. Sorry." Here she'd excited him when he was so vulnerable, and all she'd meant to do was offer him a ride. A ride home, not a sensual ride… She shook her head. Her thoughts were going down a wicked path.

Even worse, her mouth watered, wanting to relieve him right now, to lick and suck her way down that long shaft until he forgot about his pain, forgot about the rodeos he'd be missing, and thought only of her. *Naughty girl.*

"Don't be sorry." He adjusted himself, arranging

the blanket to camouflage his erection. "If we're going to be together for two days—"

"Three days. I don't want to exhaust you by making you ride in a car for ten hour days."

"Why?" His eyes dropped, heavy lidded, and his voice turned sensual. "You want me to keep up my strength for that hotel room?"

Her pussy lips tingled as flames rose inside her belly, convulsing her core and making her thighs quiver.

They stared at each other for a long, seductive minute, both of them sucking air into their lungs, both of them tense and ready.

A quick knock sounded on the door as it was opened by a staff person carrying a tray. "Dinner." The girl set the tray on a table and wheeled it to his bed then grinned at him and batted her eyes. "Is there anything else I can get you?"

Cade winked at Terri. "Any chance you have another tray out there? I promised to take this lady to dinner."

Terri bit her lips to keep from laughing. The next three days were going to be a heck of a lot of fun.

****

Terri used the key card to open the door to their fancy room and wheeled in her suitcase. She'd chosen an upscale hotel for their first night together… She rolled her eyes. Why did she just assume he'd be in the mood to make love? A girl could only hope.

Cade followed, lugging his bag and looking worn out. They'd driven five hours, chatted about everything from how close their homes were—OKC and Fort Worth—to their goals and dreams. She'd brought up the helmet topic, but he'd changed the subject. Her hard headed cowboy. They'd met with her customer over dinner where Cade was a huge hit. Now he looked ready to collapse.

"Two beds?" He set his bag on one.

She'd asked for two queen beds, just so he'd be able to rest his shoulder without her jostling him all night.

"Just because I gave you a ride and bought you supper," she teased. "I don't expect you to put out."

He laughed and tossed his Stetson on the dresser. Yawning, he sat on the bed. "I may not have the energy to put out." His eyelids drooped. "That pain pill is kickin' in."

"Let me get your boots off. She backed up to him and pulled his leg up between hers, yanking off the first boot. The second one came off just as easily. "Anything else I can help with?" She turned to face him.

He pulled her down on the bed next to him, falling back and moaning when his shoulder hit.

"Do you need an ice pack?"

"No," he croaked. "The pain that I have, only you can ease." His devilish grin made her go all wonky inside. She ran her fingers along his jaw. The day's growth of beard bristled under her fingertips.

"You rest for a while. I have some work to do. Then…" She leaned in for a quick kiss. "We'll talk about easing your pain."

"You're the boss."

She set his bag on the floor and Cade barely made it all the way onto the bed before his breathing turned steady and slow.

****

Six hours later, the sound of water running in the shower woke Terri. It took her a moment to gain her bearings. The water stopped. How could he be showering with one arm?

She knocked on the bathroom door. "Do you need help?"

"Yeah." His voice sounded pained.

Opening the door, a blast of steam rolled past her, scented with shampoo and soap. Her eyes shot to his perfect ass, displayed for her pleasure. Wow, he was all tight muscle and firm flesh. She wanted to touch.

Wrangling the towel over his head, he turned and smiled at her.

Her eyes locked on his face to keep herself from staring at the hard, engorged flesh at his hips. "What can I do to help?"

He pulled off the plastic bag he'd fastened over his shoulder and arm, threw it away, then grabbed the base of his cock. "I've got an ache, Terri."

God, she wanted that hard length slamming into

her. She bit her lip and walked toward him. Grabbing a dry towel, she rubbed it across his chest, down his sides, then knelt, drying his feet and calves.

When she looked up at him, his gaze bore into hers. Her face was inches from his big, pulsing cock, its plum-shaped head wet with drops from the shower, and a pearly bead of pre-cum.

Terri wasn't strong enough to resist the temptation. She lapped his head with her tongue, tasting his salty cum.

Cade growled, baring his teeth.

Running the towel between his legs, she cupped his balls in the terrycloth and rubbed. She wet her lips and slid him into her mouth and down her throat until her lips pressed against the furring of dark hair at his base.

"Fuck!" He slammed his hand against the wall.

The noise startled her and she swallowed, squeezing his head tighter inside her.

"So fucking good." He set his hand on her hair.

As she looked up at him, she eased her mouth from his cock. His face showed pure bliss. A spasm of need clutched her pussy. Taking him deep again, she trembled with the power she held over him and the rush that pleasing him gave her.

His hand played with strands of her hair as she increased her speed, added her hand to circle the base of his shaft.

When he gripped her hair in a fist, she looked up

at him, amazed at the pure sensuality in his expression and the heat in his eyes. Her butt tightened and she pressed her thighs together, writhing in an attempt to ease her own ache.

"You have to stop." He eased her mouth off of him. "I have to be inside you." Wrapping his hand around her arm, he tugged her up off the floor. He pulled her tight in a one-armed grip. His lips slanted over hers, a quick, frantic kiss where their tongues played, bit, and sucked. "Aw, sweetheart."

He turned her to face the marble countertop. The mirror reflected their images. "Shoulder feels better when I'm standing up." He grinned. "And this way, I can see every inch of you…" He kissed her neck and ran his hand under her long t-shirt. "…when I slide my cock into your hot pussy."

"Ahhh." Her head dropped back onto his good shoulder as visions of him fucking her, hard and fast, made every nerve in her body zing with electricity.

As his hand cupped her breast, his lips sucked her earlobe into his mouth. He flicked a finger across her nipple and she shuddered, needing more.

"Take this off." He tugged her shirt up and she peeled it off and threw it.

He stared at the reflection of her breasts in the mirror. "Damn it, if I wasn't so crazy to be inside you, I'd spend hours feasting on these." His hand circled her breast before he squeezed her nipple between his finger and thumb. "Beautiful." He looked into her eyes. "You're beautiful, Terri. But more than just on the outside." He looked about as surprised at the words he'd spoken as she was.

His words formed a soft cocoon around her heart, but she couldn't take time to examine the emotion. Right now, she wanted him to take her, release the pent-up tension she'd been feeling since she'd met him.

"These, too." Cade tugged at the back of her panties.

She eased the lacy undies down her legs and stepped out of them. When she straightened, her gaze caught his reflection in the mirror.

His eyes followed her belly down to the red curls between her legs. "Did I tell you," he growled, low and quiet. "I love your red hair." His hand grasped her hip, pulling her against his hard body, his stiff shaft pressing into her ass cheek.

His hand slid around to her stomach then snuck lower.

Watching him touch her, feeling his hand on her skin ramped up her desire, shot wicked blasts of heat through her core, swelling and pulsing into her cunt.

His fingers brushed through her hair, tickling and tormenting.

She reached an arm up, lacing her fingers through his wet hair while she stared at his face, watching him struggle for control, knowing he wanted to ravage her.

"Spread your legs." His voice was deep and rough.

Terri did as he commanded and was rewarded when his fingers opened her tingling pussy lips and slid along her slick folds. A trickle of her juices ran down the inside of her thigh.

His lips curled into a bad-boy smirk. "You're ready for me, aren't you, sweetheart."

"Yes—" Her breath caught as he slid a finger up into her opening, the sensual invasion sent her slit contracting and her heart skipping. "Yes, Cade. I need you now."

His body shuddered behind her and his eyes darkened to nearly black. "In my shaving kit. Get a condom."

She reached for the bag and found a box of them.

"Open it."

Her trembling fingers couldn't work fast enough but she finally had it in her hand.

"Put it on me." He eased his finger out of her cunt.

She turned and sheathed him in seconds, then turned back toward the mirror, her only thought was to get him inside her as fast as possible. Bending over, she rested her elbows on the marble, her nipples touching the cool surface, tightening them and pulling hard on the invisible connection between her breasts and her clit.

Tipping her ass higher in the air, she spread her

legs.

His eyes locked with hers, his hand grasped his cock and slid the head along her swollen slit. Easing just the head inside her, he laid his big hand on her ass cheek and squeezed.

"I have to have you..." He jerked his hips forward and entered her in one stroke.

Their moans chorused loudly, echoing through the room.

Her pussy tightened around him as her core jittered, sending thrills racing to her brain.

He withdrew nearly completely, then pushed in again, deeper this time, filling her and flooding her pussy with spasms.

Cade's teeth clenched as he withdrew and entered her, setting a pace that increased slowly, pushing his staff into her so incredibly deep and sliding out for a fraction of a second that had her need for him spiking.

As her brain began to flutter into orgasm, she pushed back into his thrusts, strafing her nipples against the marble, lifting her consciousness to another level as she shut her eyes and let the feelings take her away.

His hand found her clit and his finger rubbed, quickly and expertly. "Let go, sweetheart. Come for your cowboy."

His words, his finger, his cock driving into her, the sweet torture on her nipples, sent her flying out of her body, winging upward toward a bright light that burst into a solar blaze. Her slit contracted so hard and fast it rattled her bones. Her mind soared deep into the heat of the sun and she cried out with words that didn't make sense but made her orgasm complete.

Slowly the light faded and she fluttered back toward earth, skimming air currents that jostled her each time Cade plunged his cock into her opening.

With breaths that sounded too loud to be her own, she opened her eyes to see him reflected in the mirror, a shocked expression on his face as he eased his hand from her clit, still thrusting hard inside her. Her befuddled brain wondered if he'd come already, Had she missed it?

"Cade?"

He shook his head. "I've never seen anything as beautiful as you when you came, Terri. You're sexy and sweet and wild."

His words brought tender emotions to her eyes. "I don't think…" She chuckled. "No, I *know* I've never had an orgasm that wild before."

He looked away, then back at her. "I don't know what to say."

She frumped her brows and tried to decipher the meaning of his words. "What do you mean?"

Shaking his head, he ran his hand from her ass up along her spine and around to her stomach. His face changed back to the sexy, intense expression that turned her knees weak. With a growl, he caught her belly with his forearm and lifted her, bringing her ass higher, spreading her pussy further for his manic thrusts.

In seconds he shouted her name, his body tense and fierce, taught and feral. Pumping furiously into her, he shuddered with the force of his orgasm.

Terri had never seen anything so powerful or handsome, and her pussy clenched and spasmed in another, quick orgasm. This time, she kept her eyes open watching his reflection, ringing out her orgasm into slow pulses and tiny explosions.

A few minutes later, they made it into the bedroom and collapsed on her bed. He pulled her onto her side, facing him, his good hand playing with her hair.

Hmmm. Not the most romantic cuddler, was he.

Then his face turned serious.

Oh, shit. Her stomach soured. Had she done something wrong? She was a bulldozer, always pushing things to happen faster, always jumping from idea to idea without stopping to consider the implications. Had she forced him into something he wasn't ready for? She almost laughed at the absurdity of that thought. How many men didn't want to have crazy-hot sex with a woman who adored them? And she *did* adore him…

Oh. Holy. Shit.

Her lungs stopped working. She backed up a few inches watching his face, and hers went cold then flamed hot. What had she shouted in the bathroom?

Her eyes opened wide and she sucked in a ragged breath. "I didn't really say…"

His lips tightened and his brows furrowed. He nodded once.

Terri sat up so fast her head spun. Swinging her legs off the bed, she sat with her back to him. "I couldn't have." That wild spear of panic lodged under her heart again, and the urge to run nearly overcame her.

"You did." The bed shook as he sat up. His hand rested on her back. "You said you loved me."

She began to shake with the horror, the embarrassment. "Maybe I…" Her voice cracked on the lie. "Maybe I say that every time I come." She shook her head and dropped it into her hands. "No. That's not true. I'm sorry, I don't lie or I'd let you believe that. I'd rather have you believe that."

He sat next to her, his legs over the edge of the bed, his arm around her shoulders. "Look at me, Terri."

She shook her head, her face still pressed into her hands.

"C'mon. Talk to me."

With a sigh, she dropped her hands onto her bare thighs and turned to meet his gaze. "I've never told anyone except my parents that I love them."

"Wow. That's…" He swallowed and took a deep breath. "Then I guess this is serious."

"No, no, no." She waved her hands in her eraser

move. "It's…it just came out. I don't feel that way…" When her eyes met his, she knew she couldn't lie. "Okay, maybe I'm a little infatuated with you." She shrugged. "I've done months of research on you, watched videos, listened to interviews."

"You've been stalking me?"

Her eyes popped wide. When she saw the teasing smile and the spark in his eyes, she relaxed. "It was all for work, but…" The truth was always best. "You're an amazing guy."

He nodded. "True."

She laughed, the tension of the last few minutes eased, but didn't evaporate. "So, do you want to slow things down?" The thought of losing him because of a stupid mistake turned into a physical ache around her heart, tearing open that cocoon she'd wrapped it in earlier.

"Uh uh. No way you're getting away from me, Ms. Josephs." He laced his hand in her hair, twisted his body, and pinned her under him on the bed. "We've got two more days of travel." He kissed her nose. "One and a half more nights of extreme hotel sex." He kissed her chin. "And about a month and a half of my being unemployed and hanging around you every free second you have…"

He kissed her lips. "…to either make you come to your senses and fall out of love with me…" His face turned hard, then softened into the kind, wonderful cowboy she already knew so well. "Or to make me come to my senses and fall ass over teakettle in love with you."

Her indrawn breath was choppy with sweet, all-encompassing adoration. She bit her lip and smiled.

He laughed. "Uh oh."

He may be hard headed, but she was a bulldozer. They both knew exactly which direction this relationship was headed.

~~~~
~~~~

High Country Ride

Nikki Burlington pulled her rental car up to the ranch house, grabbed her purse, and stepped out. The scent of the pure Colorado air cleared her mind and soothed away her stress.

"Nikki?"

She turned to see a filthy cowboy strolling toward her, loose jointed and sexy. She closed her car door and nodded. This sure didn't look like the boy she'd known in high school. "Brodie?" Nearly six feet tall and lean-muscled, Brodie Layton had grown up very nicely.

His gaze ranged down her body and a slice of insecurity pierced her stomach. She'd worn her favorite pink t-shirt, the one that emphasized her breasts and small waist, and her skinny jeans that showed off her gym-sculpted butt and legs. She could almost hear him thinking that she'd grown up, too. Did he like what he saw?

He tugged the brim of his dusty hat. "Yes, ma'am." He looked at his hand then at his body. "Just rode in." He gestured behind her to the barn, the lush green field behind it spreading for miles until it butted against the foothills of the Rocky Mountains. Their snowcapped peaks captured the last rays of the summer sun. "We're digging postholes."

She'd like nothing better than to reach out to

shake his hand, touch him the way she'd longed to do all those years ago. But he was a mess, and he'd probably think she was a little crazy for wanting to get her hand dirty. She smiled and glanced back at the mountains. "It's beautiful here." The wistful tone of her voice surprised her. Her family hadn't ridden up into the Rockies in a decade. Not since her mom divorced her dad, and moved her brother and her to New York.

He pulled a red cloth out of his pocket. "Is your brother coming separate?" He wiped his hands on his bandana.

She shook her head and popped the trunk with her key fob. "He's not going to make it. Last minute emergency at his office." The asshole. The only part of the last will and testament he'd been interested in was how much he'd get out of the estate.

He stopped a few feet away. "You don't want to postpone?"

"My flight was non-refundable." She walked to the back of the car. "I don't think he's much interested, anyway. Even though he knows the exact spot dad was talking about." Tugging her duffle out of the trunk, she jumped when his hand touched hers on the handle.

"You can depend on me, Nikki." Their eyes met. "I'll get you there and back safely."

Despite the layer of grime on his face, his blue eyes caught her attention. Nearly the same color as the twilight sky, they held a depth that drew her in. The confidence he radiated told her without words that she could count on this man in a way she never could with her father or brother.

"Thanks." Her voice cracked. She glanced at his hand half covering hers. His calluses chafed her skin in a sexy, manly reassurance. Easing her hand from under his, she risked one more glance at those eyes. A skitter of awareness launched through her, tightening her nipples.

She'd gotten the basics on Brodie from her father's lawyer. He'd never married, and although he'd dated some, there'd been no one special recently.

"Good to see you again, Nikki." His voice rumbled like distant thunder. "Anything else?"

"Hm?" Yes, she wanted something else. Those full lips of his pressed against hers. That cord-muscled body pulling her in tight. A shiver of longing ripped down her spine.

"I meant…" He grinned, his teeth sparkling white in his grungy face. "Anything else in the trunk."

She turned from his mesmerizing smile and looked at the box in the trunk, sobering. "Just Dad's ashes." Picking up the small box, she tucked it inside her purse.

Brodie removed his hat and tipped his head down. "I'm sorry for your loss, Nikki." The sun glinted off his short, golden hair.

Such a gentleman. She'd missed the small

Colorado town where she'd been born and spent the first fifteen years of her life. Folks said "Howdy," and cowboys tipped their hats and held open doors for ladies. But mostly, she missed her dad. She hadn't seen him much in the last ten years. When he'd died last fall, she felt like she'd lost a part of herself.

"Thank you, Brodie. I've come to terms with it over the last six months. I'm ready to spread his ashes as he asked. Put some closure on my grief." Holy heck, why was she hanging out her personal laundry?

He glanced at her. "It's gotta be hard to lose a parent. I'm hopin' you'll find what you need up there." He gestured toward the mountains where the evening stars began popping in the darkening sky.

She hoped so, too. A yawn snuck up on her. "Sorry, long drive."

He stepped back and gestured toward the river where small log cabins stood like Monopoly houses. "Let's get you settled for the night. Morning'll come early."

****

She rambled around the cute little guest cottage preparing for the two-day ride and watching the lights go on and off in the big ranch house. It made her feel kind of lonely. With only her brother, who had no time for her, and her mother, who had a new husband and house upstate to keep her busy, Nikki spent a lot of time alone. Her work schedule didn't leave room for dating or even close friends. Another light went on. Was that his bedroom? She wished she had enough courage to go traipsing up there and ask if he wanted company. But, he lived with his parents, so that wasn't going to happen.

At six the next morning, her phone alarm woke her. She took a shower, dried her long, strawberry blonde hair, and braided it.

A knock sounded at her door. Nikki grabbed her saddlebags, set her cowgirl hat on her head, and swung open the door as she pulled on her coat.

The sun hadn't come up yet, but the light from her cabin spotlighted a sexy, clean cowboy holding a giant paper cup in one hand.

Under his brown cowboy hat, his face was outrageously handsome without all the dirt. Her breath caught in her lungs. High cheekbones and dimples popped when he smiled. Yummy. She remembered him from the few times he came to town all those years ago. He was one of the home-school kids that lived up in the mountains and got snowed in for most of the winter. He'd grown into a gorgeous hunk of cowboy.

"Black?"

Staring into those sweet blue eyes, her thoughts scattered. "Huh?"

He handed her the cup then reached both hands into the pockets of his denim jacket and produced a couple of creamers from one and a dozen pouches of sugar from the other. "How do you like your coffee?"

he enunciated with a sly grin. "Am I hard to understand with my hillbilly accent?"

She shook her head. "Sorry. Not awake yet. Black is fine. Thank you." Glancing down, her gaze caught on the impressive bulge behind the zipper of his worn jeans, then quickly dropped lower to his scuffed boots. She was evidently awake enough to have wicked thoughts about dragging him into her cabin, though.

"Horses are saddled." He stepped back to let her walk out the door, closed it behind her, and took her arm to help her down the two steps. "We'll have breakfast on the trail."

Peeking up at him through her lashes, she said, "When I made the reservations, I did mention I hadn't been on a horse in ten years. You're not going to kill me the first day, are you?"

"No, ma'am. We'll stop when you get tender."

Being this close to a big, rugged cowboy was making her tender. Tender, quivery, and very hot inside.

When she'd finished her coffee, they mounted up, following a well-worn trail along the tree line as the sun peeked up above the mountains. A clamoring of construction noise sounded in the distance.

He stopped as they topped a rise and looked down at a lush, green valley where a huge house stood near the river. The skeleton of a barn teemed with laborers.

"What a perfect place to build a house."

He dismounted. "Best spot on the ranch." He held her reins as she slid her leg over the saddle and jumped down.

Her muscles were sore, but not screaming as she sat on the boulder overlooking the peaceful scene. She'd missed Colorado. Moving from a small mountain town to a cram-packed city had been a difficult adjustment. The worst part had been leaving behind her friends. They'd just gotten to that age where they were really noticing boys.

Brodie sat next to her and handed her an egg sandwich, somehow miraculously still hot, and the cap from his thermos, full of coffee.

"Brodie?"

"Uh huh?"

"Do you remember me from when I lived here?"

He nodded, a slight smile curling his lips. "I noticed you once or twice when you were a kid, then one day you kind of…" He held out his hands, palms in, in front of his chest.

She laughed. "Yes, I developed fast once I hit fourteen."

"Yeah, you sure did." He scuffed his boot on the grass, silent for a moment. "I kinda had a thing for you." He glanced into her eyes. "Then you disappeared."

The heartache of that horrible time raced up to swamp her. She focused on the good times. "My childhood here were the best years of my life."

Swallowing back a sigh, she took a bite and chewed. The salty maple-smoked taste of fresh country ham was a local delicacy. She'd never found anything as delicious in New York.

"You're here now." One side of his mouth curved up. "And I'm real glad you are."

God, he was sweet. She was real glad to be here, too, especially on the trail with him. But the thought of leaving it all behind again in nine days brought a hollow feeling to her chest. Shaking her head to banish the gloom, she asked, "So whose is it? The house, I mean."

"Mine."

She looked at him. He'd said it so casually, she didn't know whether to believe him or not.

"My sister and her husband have a place on the far side of the folks' house, on the same river, so I claimed this land for myself."

"Wow. Do you live there now?" It didn't look occupied.

He chewed for a few seconds. "Naw. Not for another couple weeks. They're waiting for some parts for the house, then…" He grinned at her. "I need to find someone to help me furnish it."

She rolled her eyes. "And did you have anyone in mind?" Nikki graduated a year ago with her interior design degree, and worked as an unpaid intern at a prestigious agency in midtown Manhattan.

"Well," he refilled their shared coffee cup. When

he took a sip, she noticed he'd placed his lips exactly where she'd had hers. The intimacy jingled through her.

"If you have a day or so after this trail ride, I'd greatly appreciate your help." He glanced at her. "I'd pay you for your time, of course."

She sighed and stared down at the big, rambling structure. Furnishing a real house. Not a penthouse, condo, apartment, or studio, but an honest country home. "I'd do it for free."

"Couldn't let you do that." He handed her the coffee. "You're paying me to do my job. I'll pay you to do yours."

This would be fun. She had so few days to spend in Colorado. Two days on the trail to spread her father's ashes, two days packing his things and contracting with a realtor to sell his house. Spending a few days helping a sexy cowboy buy a bed would be… A chill of desire raced through her. "Okay. It's a deal."

"Good." He stood. "I brought the house plans along. We can look at them tonight." His smile was a little naughty. "Before we turn in."

When she stood, her tightening thigh muscles caused her to stumble a bit.

"Whoa, there." He reached out and grasped her arm, his big hand going around her little bicep with ease. He didn't let her go.

She looked up into his eyes.

Blue flame burned in them, dark and needy, his pupils dilated as she watched and his grip tightened, pulling her closer to him.

Not one to waste time, especially when she only had a few days, she stepped toe to toe with the sexy cowboy and lifted her lips to brush his.

Brodie grabbed her tight against him, slanting his mouth on hers, deepening the kiss, his tongue exploring her, guiding hers into his mouth to do the same. Against her belly, his hardening cock branded her.

He was the one to stop, to pull away, breathing hard. He turned his head toward his house. All sound had ceased.

Suddenly, a chorus of cheers, yee-haws, and "Bro-dies" erupted.

Brodie grimaced. "Sorry about that."

She smiled. "It's fine. At least we were PG-13."

His jaw set. "Maybe we could heat that rating up a bit, Miss Nikki." His voice growled, low and sexy. "That is, if you've a mind to."

How she'd love to. Every inch of her skin tingled, her pussy vibrated, her breasts swelled and peaked. A nine-day hookup with a devil of a cowboy would be heaven. But the thought of her father's ashes riding along in her saddlebag cooled her a bit.

"Ask me again after we set up camp?"

He laughed. "I will. You can count on it." He gathered the remains of breakfast and got them back on the trail in minutes. The day sped by as they climbed steadily upward. They stopped twice, just long enough to let the horses drink, have themselves a snack and a stretch, and enjoy a long, lingering kiss.

They learned about each other as they rode side by side. She was surprised by the pristine beauty of the land and his love for it. Just as the sun set, they reached the creek where her father wanted his ashes sprinkled. While Brodie set up camp, Nikki wandered downstream and spent a quiet half hour scattering her father's ashes. She felt her dad lingering along the riverbank and in the pine forest behind her and spoke quietly to his spirit.

When she walked back into camp, Brodie set down the hatchet he was using to split wood. Pulling her into his arms, he asked, "How are you doin'?"

She nodded. "It's good. I feel….settled."

"Good." His hand on her back stroked along her spine. "Anything I can do?"

"Mmmm." *Keep touching me like this.* Her heart thudded, loving his kindness, his need to help her. She pulled back. "I'm starving. Feed me?"

Over a crackling fire, Brodie cooked them a dinner of hamburgers and mac and cheese. Sitting next to each other on a log, their legs touched from hip to knee and a frantic heat flowed through her veins, keeping her warmer than the fire could. They feasted on apple pie made fresh by his mother, feeding each other forkfuls followed by kisses that tasted like cinnamon.

As he washed dishes, she reviewed the house plans and asked him a hundred questions. Finally, he dried his hands and leaned over behind her looking at the plans and answering another dozen questions.

With an exasperated sigh, he wrapped his arms around her and nibbled on her neck, sending her latest question about the house scattering from her brain.

He tipped her back, his mouth pressing against hers as his fingers brushed her cheek. His kiss sent her spinning, his lips hot and firm, his tongue plunging, setting a rhythm that her hips couldn't help but follow.

"Any more questions?" His grin was pure seduction.

"As if I could remember after that kiss." She fanned herself with the papers. "Go back to your dishes so I can finish studying the blueprints."

He laughed but did as she requested.

Putting this place together for Brodie would be a pleasure, but with the lead time on furniture, she'd probably never see it completed. Maybe he'd invite her back for a visit? Leaving Colorado again would be difficult, but leaving Brodie just when they'd begun to connect—that would be dismal.

When everything was packed away and made bear-safe, he carried their bedrolls beside the fire. "Nice night," he growled, low and sexy.

"Uh huh." Her belly did a sensual flip. "Might be

fun to stay outside a while longer." Her reservations about letting herself go tonight had melted away as soon as she'd said her last goodbye to her dad.

His grin flashed in the firelight. "I'm thinkin' the same thing."

She licked her lips, suddenly wanting him with a ravenous desire.

He unrolled their sleeping bags and laid them one atop the other. "Come over here."

She stood. The deep rumble of his voice lit a flare of desire that overpowered her and set her knees to wobble. Her pussy flooded with cream. She walked toward him and he took her hand.

He turned her to face the river, her back pressed against his chest. "Look." He pointed to a clearing in the trees. Over the mountain peaks, a sliver of a moon hung in the star speckled sky.

"Beautiful," she whispered, soaking it into her memory.

"You don't get this in New York City."

She smiled a little sadly. "No. You sure don't." A few yards away, the river trickled sleepily. Crickets chirruped and a night bird called.

His lips touched her ear. "I had a dream about you last week."

His warmth soaked into her body and his words wound through her heart. "What was it about?"

"Mmmm." His teeth nibbled along the ridge of her ear. "I'll tell you later."

Rivulets of desire flowed from her ear down to her needy flesh. Her breasts swelled and peaked, her core shuddered, and her thighs tingled.

"I want you, Nikki." He proved it by pressing his hard cock against her backside. "I can't think straight from needing you so bad."

She wanted this desperately. She nearly stumbled as she turned toward him. Her nipples brushed against his chest, sending skitters down low to her clit.

Setting her hands on his chest, she brushed the softest of kisses on his lips. "I'm yours, Brodie."

"I hope you mean that."

If his words had a deeper meaning, she couldn't grasp it with her brain focusing fully on what their bodies wanted. Unbuttoning his shirt, she scratched her nails gently through the golden hair, down low to where his belt buckle gleamed in the fire, highlighting the massive bulge beneath it.

Something clicked and they both went for each other's clothes, unzipping, unbuttoning, and tugging everything off, throwing it in a pile.

"You're beautiful," he breathed, just looking at her, from her face down to her breasts, and lower to her bare pussy. "Perfection."

She looked at him in the glow of the fire, his body hard and lean, his cock standing long and proud. Her mouth watered, wanting a taste. Needing to show him how much she desired him, how much she… What? She wanted him, yes, but there was something more.

Something quiet and consuming. Glancing up into his eyes, she noticed the condom packet he held between his teeth, his grin turned wicked.

"So you were pretty sure you'd get lucky, huh?" A flash of lust raced down her spine.

"A cowboy is prepared for anything."

"Anything?" She knelt on the sleeping bags, grasping his hard staff in her hand. "Even this?" Licking his head, she tasted salty pre-cum.

He jerked and groaned, his body tightening.

She took him all, quick and tight before pulling her lips off him then taking him deep again.

Brodie laced his fingers in her hair, his breathing uneven. "Nikki, sweetheart, I'm gonna have to ask you to stop or I might just…" He shuddered as she grasped his balls and slowly eased her lips from his base to his head. "I wanna be deep in your sweet pussy when I come."

The rumble of his seductive words made her slit quiver as she imagined easing down onto his cock, filling herself.

Kneeling in front of her, he kissed her, his hands caressing her breasts, toying with her nipples. Against her lips, he whispered, "You wanna ride for a while?"

How could he know her favorite position? "Was that what you saw in your dream?"

He nodded. "You in the firelight." He shivered. "Riding fast and hard."

She wasn't sure about fast or hard, but she needed

him inside her. "Lay down, cowboy," she purred.

He complied, handing her the condom as he laced his hands behind his head in a deceptively casual pose. His eyes burned and his teeth gritted. He was as wild to have her as she was to impale herself on his big shaft.

Sheathed and stiff, he lay still, offering himself to her. "Take it, Nikki. Take it all."

Nikki would have everything he could give. But slowly. Sensually. Pressing her nipples to his chest, she slid his cock along the length of her dripping pussy lips.

"Driving me crazy. Stop teasing," he moaned and moved his hands from behind his head.

She grasped them, pushing them down onto their makeshift bed. "Uh uh. Let me lead, Brodie."

He chuckled, dark and sinful. "I'll let you run *this* show. But the next round, you'll learn who's boss."

Her core contracted just thinking about him taking control, holding *her* down. But she wouldn't concede that easily. Arching her back, she brought her slit to the tip of his cock. It pulsed, hot and ready, tickling her, taunting her.

Circling her hips, she made a seductive game out of taking him higher, feeling her own need reaching the breaking point.

Jerking upward, he tried to push his length into her opening.

"Uh uh, cowboy. I'm the boss, remember?" She'd

make him wait a little longer. Make the moment sweeter.

His body tensed. "You're making me nuts, woman," he groaned.

"Good," she whispered. "Then you'll love this." Bending over, she sucked his nipple and nibbled it, still touching just the head of his erection with her opening.

"Fuck this," he roared as he sat up and grasped her hips, pushing her onto his cock with one strong thrust.

She screamed with pleasure as her pussy contracted around him, her core quivered as he filled her deeply, stretching her, the bliss more intense than she'd ever known.

With his cock still inside her, he lifted her and laid her on her back, holding her ass in his big hands as he knelt.

She wrapped her legs around his waist. As blood rushed to her head, she let go of everything and let him take her, let him take charge.

His strokes became faster, deeper, and she spread herself for him, wanting to have him all, every inch of him.

His fingers found her clit and he circled, rubbed, pinched, until a wild orgasm overtook her, flinging her upward toward the star-studded sky, rolling her through the rarified air until all she could do was feel and fly.

Brodie's shouts joined hers as his hips pounded into hers, his cock thickened, the friction heating her from the inside. With a last shudder, he collapsed next to her and pulled her close.

For minutes they just panted, taking turns quivering with aftershocks. His fingers trailed along her stomach, up to her breasts. "I didn't get time to taste these," he groaned. Sliding his hand down to her mound, he cupped it. "Or this."

His touch wound up the spring inside her that he'd unraveled just seconds ago. "Fantastic." It was all she could say and only a tiny portion of what she felt. Connected, happy, secure, content.

Propping his head on his bent arm, he looked down at her. "Yeah. Fucking fantastic, Nikki." One rough finger eased its way between her swollen pussy lips and stroked gently. "This next time it'll be outrageous." He grinned.

The firelight flickering across his face turned him more handsome, more rugged than ever. She wanted this, with him, all night. "And the time after that?" she asked. "Unbelievable?"

He lifted his finger from her pussy to his mouth and licked. "How about, 'delicious'?"

Her core heated and convulsed, wanting him again, hard and fast, soft and slow, any way she could get him.

"We've got all night to pull off each one of those," she breathed heavily, holding her lust back with intense concentration. "And eight more days." She grinned. "If you don't wear me out completely."

His brow creased and he tensed. "Eight days?"

Why was he surprised? "Yes. Until I go home."

"Home?" He sat up, looking down on her. "Aren't you moving into your dad's place?"

She propped herself on her elbows. "I'm packing his things and finding a realtor. Then I'm going back to New York." The idea of leaving Colorado, leaving Brodie, sent painful tugs at her heart.

"Shit." He fell back on the sleeping bags, staring up into space. "Rumor was that you were moving here. Permanently."

Placing her hand on his chest, she sighed. "I looked into opening a design firm here in town, but I'd have to spend every penny of my savings as well as my inheritance to do it."

He wouldn't look at her.

"I can't risk losing everything." She sat up and wrapped her arms around her legs. Suddenly the evening air curled around her, chilling her flesh.

He sat up next to her. "Sure you can."

"What?" She looked into his eyes.

Brodie gazed at her with expectant excitement. "People do it every day. Start businesses." He gestured toward town. "You could get a small business loan. After you decorate my house, we'll have a party to show it off and round up some business for you." He took her braid in his hand and ran his fingers down its length, tickling her chin with the end. "There's lot of new construction hereabouts."

It had been her dream, to open her own business. Her father's house sat squarely on main street. If she could get a variance to office out of it, she wouldn't have to pay rent for a storefront. It would be heaven to live in a real house with windows facing the Rockies. In New York, her tiny studio apartment had one window that faced a the brick wall of the next building.

"Unless…" He dropped her braid. "Is there someone in New York? A man?" His eyes narrowed and his jaw tightened.

It struck her, then. He'd been asking about her around town and finding out what her plans were. He'd started a relationship today that he intended would last for more than nine days. Who was this amazing cowboy?

She reached over and touched his forearm. "No. There's no one. Not in New York." Could she tell him with her eyes that her "someone" lived right here?

He brushed the backs of his fingers over her cheek. "You'll consider it?"

Nikki tried to read the meaning in his intense stare. Did he want her to consider a future with him?

"I'm considering it."

He settled her butt between his legs, both of them facing the crackling fire.

She leaned back and kissed his jaw. "And it's

feeling more right by the minute."

"Good." Brodie tipped his head and looked into her eyes. "I'm…mighty fond of you, Nikki."

His admission warmed her from the inside out. It was too soon to make promises or commitments, but she would seriously rethink her plans. She snuggled back into his arms. "Would you be willing to…" She moved his hand to her breast. "…do a little more convincing?"

His laugh filled the night, and rumbled against her back, ricocheting through her. Cupping both her breasts, he whispered hot in her ear, "If I only have eight days to convince you to stay, I'd better get to work."

As his fingers plucked her nipples, she went boneless and closed her eyes. "Did I mention, cowboy?" She sucked in an uneven breath. "I'm mighty fond of you, too."

~ ~ ~ ~

Kill Me or Kiss Me

Paige Randolph adjusted the air vent on her red vintage Camaro as she roared down the desolate gravel road. The near-full moon glowed over acres of Hill Country ranch land spread out on both sides of her.

She yawned, tired after her late shift at the Naked Cowgirl in Austin. The cool outside air coming into the car kept her awake but a strand of her long platinum hair blew up into her eyes. Her tires nearly left the ground as she sped over a rise in the road.

Directly in front of her, a semi sat right in the middle of the road. "Oh, damn!" Slamming on the brakes, she realized her mistake when her car slid sideways. Turning the wheel, she let up on the brakes and barely missed the front of the truck. The ditch caught her front end. The Camaro's back end slid down the embankment and stopped with her headlights facing the road.

When the dust settled, Paige held up her hands, watching them shake. Close call. That could have been really bad.

Beyond her fingertips, where her headlights shone on the back of the truck, a cow stared at her.

Why would the Royal T Ranch be moving cattle in the middle of the… "Rustlers." Her heart palpitated a couple times. Shit, what should she do?

Dropping the gearshift into low, she pressed the gas pedal, praying for traction. Her tires spun. When she glanced up at the truck, five men walked toward her. Each of them wore all black except for the random colored bandanas they'd pulled over the lower half of their faces.

"Crap, crap, crap." Without looking down, she stuck her right hand into her purse, fumbling for her phone. Her night's cash tips flew out of her bag as she furiously searched and…found it. She pressed the unlock button and touched "Dial."

Someone tapped on her window. She rolled it down an inch and forced a smile. "Hi. Sorry, I didn't see your truck—"

"Get out." The low voice chilled her.

"Actually, if y'all would give me a push, I'd—"

"Out." This time, the barrel of a pistol peeked in her window.

Fear raced through her, tightening her chest and making her whole body hot. What were her options? She could dial 911 and hope the gun was just a threat. She moved her phone closer.

"You try it, sugar, and I'll have to shoot off your hand."

She looked up at him, a large shape in the darkness. His voice told her he was serious. How would she do either of her jobs with a missing hand? She dropped her phone.

"Turn off the engine."

She did as he asked, plunging them into darkness. When he opened the car door, the interior lights popped on. She looked down at the steep grade. Thankfully, she'd changed from her six-inch platform heels into her flip-flops, but navigating the incline was not going to be easy.

A flashlight beam from the road blinded her. She held up a hand to shade her eyes.

"She's pretty," a different rustler said.

She hadn't taken off her stage makeup, planning to take a shower once she got home.

The light dropped lower to her big D breasts. She'd also opted out of a bra and panties when she'd put on her tank top and shorts. Now, her choices had left her open for something worse than getting her hand shot off. Her stomach pitched at the thought.

"Back off," a third voice said. This one was forceful and confident.

"If you're so worried about her, Buck, you get her out of there." It was the gunman's voice.

"Good idea to use my name, asshole," Buck replied.

"Ahh. It ain't your real name anyways. Climb down there and bring her up onto the road."

The sound of boots scrabbling down a rocky incline told her Buck was on his way.

A face appeared, a bandana across his nose, mouth, and chin, a baseball cap pulled down low. She caught a glimpse of black hair and green eyes in the dashboard lights. "Ma'am. No one's going to hurt you if you cooperate."

"Right. Like I haven't heard that line in the movies. Just before they strangle the heroine."

He chuckled then took her by the waist and hefted her out of the car as if she were a blow-up doll. He slung her arm over his head and picked her up in a fireman's carry.

At a hefty one-fifty and five-foot eleven, she wasn't a little thing. Curvy, the other girls at the club called her, and it sure helped bring in the tips when she danced.

His hand rested on her bare thigh, his thumb touching her soft inner-leg, easing close to where her short shorts ended. "Hold on."

Hanging upside down, she had no idea what to hang on to. She wrapped her arms around his waist, her hands laying flat on a nice bunch of firmness hiding under his dark shirt. As he muscled his way up the incline, she felt his abs straining, his back flexing, hard and hot.

"Jeez." She rolled her eyes. She was just about to be raped or killed or both, and she was thinking about man flesh? For once, her mom had been right. She felt like a tramp.

Her human pack mule reached the dirt road but didn't put her down. "What are we gonna do with her?"

"I get her first," the guy who thought she was

pretty said.

The man under her turned. "Uh uh. We're not addin' rape to cattle rustlin'. If we get caught, that'll add ten years to our sentence."

"Caught?" The gunman laughed. "We been doing this for three years and ain't been caught." He cleared his throat. "But you're right. I ain't no rapist."

A couple men started to argue, but Gunman said, "Get back to work. We've got another half hour at least." He grumbled something that sounded like, lazy fuckers. "Buck, tie her up."

Buck bent over and set her on her feet. The rush of blood from her head spun her brain and she stepped back to keep from toppling. She considered running, but in her flip flops versus his six-foot-six body and long legs in combat boots, she didn't stand a chance.

His big hand grabbed her forearm. "You okay?"

She nodded. As okay as a girl could be while facing her own death. As her eyes adjusted to the moonlight, she looked up at him. His baseball cap had fallen off. Above his bandana, his eyes shone emerald green, fringed with long, black lashes. She glanced away quickly. She didn't want to possess any descriptions that would make these guys decide she would be better off a dead witness, than a live one.

He leaned close. "Listen, I'll make sure you're not hurt. Just stay quiet. Okay?"

His words gave her hope. She could survive this

night, either with his help, or on her own.

Buck pressed his palm on the hood of her car. "Lean up against the grill."

"Why?"

He huffed out a quick laugh. "Because I told you to," he enunciated. "And I've got the gun." He lifted his shirt, revealing a small black pistol tucked into the waistband of his pants.

Shit. She should have felt him up a little more. She could have grabbed it and…aw, hell, she didn't know how to shoot a pistol.

"Christ, girl, are you slow or what?" He lifted her by the waist, and leaned her against her car.

He was strong. Their eyes met, and a surge of something wicked sent a chill through her.

He released her immediately and stepped back. "What the hell were you doing racing down a minimum maintenance road at three in the morning?" He pulled out a zip tie and fastened it around her ankles.

She loved listening to his voice. Low and mellow. The brush of his fingers on her bare ankles ramped up her awareness. "I always race down this road at three in the morning." She pointed toward her little hobby farm on the river. "I live down there at the dead end…" Her eyes opened wide. She hefted out a sigh as she dropped her head into her hands. "Real stupid, Paige," she mumbled. She had to learn to keep her mouth shut.

He chuckled. "Is this your first time being held hostage?"

She looked up at him and grimaced. "How can you tell?"

"Arms out." He held the other zip tie. "You've kind of got a certain thing going on."

She held out her arms, wrists together. "Dumb blonde?"

He shrugged. "You said it, I didn't."

"Buck! Get over here you lazy fuck!" It sounded like Gunman's voice.

"Guess that's me." He took a step away then said over his shoulder, "Don't make any trouble."

He jogged back to where the men wrangled cattle up a ramp into the truck. The lowing sounds of the beasts tugged at her heart. The Royal T was a cow and calf operation. These men were taking mommas away from their babies. The cows wouldn't sell for half as much as steers would. She snapped her fingers and did a head swing. "And they call me dumb."

After five minutes struggling with the zip ties, she'd only managed to chafe her skin. There was no chance she could hop away from them. Her house was a mile away. She'd have to figure another plan to get out of this mess. She'd seen where Buck kept his gun. Next time he got close, could she grab it and bluff her way to freedom?

Within fifteen minutes, the truck was ready to roll. The men walked toward her, a line of menacing black shapes. Oh, shit. Her stomach churned.

Buck picked her up and set her near the semi trailer. "We're going to push your car out."

Gunman got behind the wheel and started the engine. The others slid down into the ditch and stood behind the car.

Buck gestured down the road in the direction their truck was pointed. "About a mile that way, there's a mailbox. I'll leave your keys and phone in there."

She nodded, hoping it was all coming to an end. That it was just that simple. "Okay."

Gunman gave the Camaro gas and the other three grunted as they pushed. The car gained about a foot, then sunk back down again, sending the men scrambling out of the way.

"Stupid fuckers." He looked at her. "Have you got a jacket in the car? It's getting cold."

"Yes. I'll be fine." She glanced at him. "Thank you. I appreciate it."

"Just try to…" He rubbed his forehead. "I've got sisters. And if I caught them driving hell-for-leather down a dirt road, or wearing next to nothing." He glanced down her body. "I'd pack them off to boarding school."

His words touched a part of her soul that had long since gone into hiding. "That's…" What was she going to say? That's sweet of you to care about me? He didn't care. He was just a cattle thief, hoping she'd forget the color of his eyes when she talked to the sheriff.

The second try getting the car out was just as unsuccessful. Buck jogged over and took another guy's place at the back of the car.

The man who thought she was pretty climbed out of the ditch and walked up to her. Even by the weak light of the moon, she could see the rancid lust in his eyes. "Cut you loose, cutie?"

She held out her hands.

He snapped on the flashlight and shined it at her hands…and her breasts. "Too pretty to waste," he mumbled. The beam traced down her belly, stopping at her mound, then slid down her legs. "Fuck if I'm not hard and ready. Wanna lay down on the hood of your little red car and let me give you a good hard pounding?" His hand snaked out and twisted her nipple. "Fifty bucks."

She batted his hand away and hopped back. "Not for fifty million, cow stealer."

The Camaro's engine roared. Within seconds, it was out of the ditch, and parked facing her house.

Flashlight Guy laughed. "I could take it for free, pretty girl." He shined the flashlight in her face. "Hey, I know you. You're a stripper at the Naked Cowgirl."

The other men walked up behind him.

"Shut. Up." Buck put his baseball cap on backward. Was he talking to Flashlight or her?

Things clicked in her head. Flashlight Guy's voice, his slimy leer. "You're the bastard who beat the crap out of Misti, aren't you." She hopped forward and slammed her fists into his chest. "The sheriff is looking for..." Oh, shit, shit, shit. Why did she always have to open her stupid mouth?

Buck rubbed his forehead and sighed.

The other men stared at her as if she were the last sacrificial virgin.

Gunman pulled out his weapon. "Well, we've got no choice, now."

"Hold on here," Buck said, moving between the pistol and her. "She doesn't know for sure who this guy is." He turned to her. "Right, blondie?"

She took his meaning: be a dumb blonde. "I don't know him." She thought fast. "And you know where I live, and where I work. I'd be stupid to call the sheriff." Her whole body shook with fear.

Silence.

The air sparked with tension.

"We can't take that chance," Gunman said, sliding a bullet into the chamber.

"Not here." Buck looked at each of the men. "Let me do her."

Do her? Her stomach threatened to empty.

"That's right." Gunman clicked his gun and put it away. "We have a cold blooded killer with us this trip."

Buck laughed. "Damn right. And I know what I'm doing. They've never been able to make a case against me." He turned and grabbed her arm. "I'll make blondie's death look accidental."

"Is that how you did those other women?" Gunman asked.

"Yeah." He pulled her close and tugged off his bandana. His mouth curved into a cruel smile. "This one'll be easy." His eyes narrowed, flashing evil. "Who's going to question a hooker dying of a drug and alcohol overdose?"

Her mouth opened then shut with a clamp of teeth. She was an exotic dancer. Not a hooker. But who the hell cared now, when she was facing her last hours. She tried to jerk her arm out of his grip. He wasn't letting her go.

Okay, she wasn't dead yet. She had to think. What were her options? Sweet talk? Play dumb until she found her chance? Go on the offensive?

"All right. Load up, shitheads," Gunman ordered. "Buck, make it quck."

"I'll have everything done and cleaned up in a couple hours."

"We'll meet at that bar in three days." Gunman laughed as he walked past them. "Have fun with her."

"Yeah," Flashlight Guy said. "Give her one in the ass for me." He squeezed her butt on his way past.

The truck rumbled to life and shifted into gear, pulling away from them.

She had to do something before he got her into her car. Into her house. Ducking her head, she did a dolphin-kind of launch right toward his face. Her forehead connected with his nose.

He stumbled back. "Aw, fucking son of a…"

Paige hopped like a frantic bunny toward her car. She lost a flip-flop on the way, but the gravel biting into her foot gave her the extra incentive to make this happen. Expecting to be tackled from behind at any second, she surprised herself by reaching the car. Opening the door, she clambered in.

After slamming the door, she pressed down the old-fashioned lock button and reached her captive hands toward the ignition. Nothing there. "Crap, crap, crap." She looked around the floor, the passenger seat, the cup holders.

Metal tapping sounded on the window.

She looked up.

Buck stood there, blood running from both nostrils, her keys in his hand.

****

Before Stripper Girl could hold down the door lock, Slade Keating, A.K.A. "Buck," used the key to unlock it. He pulled open the door. "You're not in any—"

She kicked out at him with her bound feet, missing his genitals by an inch.

His nose hurt like hell, throbbing through his whole face. He wasn't in the mood for any more games. "Listen to me, or I'm going to throw you in the trunk." He punctuated that statement by shaking his finger at her. Christ, he was behaving like his dad tonight.

"No." She jumped out and came at him, trying to gut punch him with her head.

He stepped aside easily.

She lost her balance and started to fall. "Oh, crap."

"Yeah." He grabbed her with one arm around the waist. "Crap is right." He hauled her to the trunk and opened with the key. He stood her up and grabbed her hair, gently, just to keep her from head butting him again. "You wanna listen? Or you want in the trunk?"

She clamped her proud little jaw tight and pursed those pink, pouty lips. His hand in her hair felt the thickness, softness, of her long tresses. The moon's light practically set it glowing. Those dark, sexy eyes pierced him. "I'll listen." She glanced away, her perfect face set obstinately.

He'd never been much for blondes, but he'd make an exception in her case. He glanced away, willing his cock to stop jumping around to get his attention. This was work, not play.

"I'm not a hooker." She looked at him with venom in her eyes. "I dance topless. I don't prostitute myself."

A snort tried to come out his nose, but only pain resulted. His lip curled. "You think you're about to die, and all you care about is making me believe you're not a whore?"

She gritted her teeth and moved toward him,

threatening.

He tugged on her hair, stopping her. "You're not going to die. I'm a Texas Ranger working undercover to catch the head honcho of this rustling gang."

She stood completely still for a moment. Her chest didn't even rise with her breaths. And he had been staring at her chest tonight. Firm, full, bouncy.

Turning from him, she swallowed hard. "Just kill me. Don't play games."

Damn stubborn woman. He pulled his knife out of his pocket and flicked it open.

She stiffened, but didn't fight.

He cut the bindings at her wrists then at her feet. Walking toward where the truck had been parked, he bent down and brought her sandal back to her. He crouched down and held it out, alert to her painful tricks but wanting to prove his motives were innocuous.

Her eyebrows drew down, but she lifted her foot and let him put the thong between her toes.

Standing, he reached in his pocket and handed her phone to her. "Call 911. Ask for Ranger Special Op Five."

She took it, but stared at him.

He backed up a dozen feet and sat on his heels. "I'm telling the truth."

The glow of her phone highlighted her face as she dialed. With the phone to her ear, she said, "Ranger Special Op Five. Please?"

After a few seconds, her eyes opened wide. "Um, hi. I'm calling for a guy who says he's a Ranger?"

"Slade Keating," he supplied.

She stared at him. "Slade Keating."

"Uh huh." She leaned back against the open trunk. "Okay." Raising her free hand, it shook as she pressed it across her eyes. "Yes, he's here. Thank you." Her voice sounded strained. Her hand holding the phone dropped to her side. "He wants to talk to you." Her voice shook. Were those tears?

Slade stood and walked to her side, taking the phone in one hand, and pulling her up against him with the other. "It's okay, darlin'."

She wrapped her arms around him, pressed her face into his shoulder, and sniffled out her relief.

He found himself rubbing her back as he explained the situation to his supervisor.

"You'll need to stay with her, Keating. Lay low. No outside contact. Two days, maybe three. Until we can apprehend the entire ring."

"I should be in on the bust, Lieutenant. She can go to a safe house—"

"No. This is your out. They'll think you escaped. We can use that."

"Right." Disappointment flooded him. He wanted to be there when they nabbed these guys.

"Don't let her out of your sight."

Tipping his head, he breathed deep of her scent. Coconut and hairspray. Kind of sexy.

"You hear me, Keating?"

"Yes sir, lieutenant."

"We show the truck heading south. If anything changes, if it circles back, I'll call you."

"Yes sir. I'll check in tomorrow." He hung up and slid her phone into his pocket.

Her crying had slowed to a trickle.

He untied his bandana and handed it to her.

She mopped up and blew her nose, then held up the cloth. "I'm guessing you don't want this back?"

He laughed. "Keep it to remind you how lucky you got tonight."

She glanced up at him, one arm wrapping around his waist again. "Thank you for what you did tonight."

"All I did was not be a murderer."

"No." She used a corner of the bandana to wipe away the blood from under his nose. "You are a hero. You risked your life to bring those men to justice. If there's ever anything I can do…"

Lacing his fingers through her luminous hair, he tipped her head back. "A reward?"

She stiffened for a second, then smiled. "A kiss for not killing me? Sounds fair."

Their lips met, hers were as juicy and soft as they looked. Running his tongue over them, he tasted cherries and mint. Her teeth were straight, and he traced them leisurely, tickling her inner lips.

He lapped her tongue, coaxing her until she

explored his mouth with her tongue. She teased him with little licks and nips. She bit his lower lip then whispered, "My house is just a mile away."

"I'll drive."

He opened her car door for her, raced to her acreage on the river, and pulled her with him into the cottage. Closing the door, he tugged her against him then backed her against the door.

"Goddamnit." He flipped on the light switch. "I don't even know your name."

She laughed, deep and happy, and ran her hands up under his shirt. "My real name or my stage name?"

"Both." He tugged off his t-shirt and tossed it.

She licked her lips as she gazed at his chest. Her fingers stroked his flesh, sending spikes of desire down low in his belly. She touched his scars, but thankfully didn't ask about them. His swirls of dark hair seemed to fascinate her. "Um…" She forced her gaze from his body. "At night, I'm Gina Colada—like piña colada? I use coconuts and pineapple in my act."

He tipped his head back and laughed. "I've got to see this."

She grimaced a little. "It pays the bills. I'm really Paige Randolph, college student, finishing my degree in website design."

"So you're not a dumb blonde?"

She lifted her shoulders. "Some days, yes." She touched her fingers to the part in her hair. I'm actually a brunette."

He looked closer. "Damned if you're not." He liked brunettes. This fascinating woman already had all his attention and half his heart. She was brave. Not a whine or tear out of her when she faced death. And a fighter. She'd damn near knocked him out. If he hadn't thought to grab the car keys, she'd have been long gone. "You've got a lot of little secrets."

"Listen—Buck?" She grinned.

"Yes, Ms. Colada?" He smirked.

"I need to shower." She sniffed. "And you could probably use one, too."

"Rustling cows will do that to a man."

She stepped around him. "I'll be right out."

"Uh uh." He grabbed her from behind and pulled her cute, round bottom against his hard cock. "We can do this together…" He looked past her. "Aw, shit. Is that a pole?"

She pushed his arms from around her and stepped away. "It's not what you think. It's just for practicing."

"No, it's great. I mean, I have a virtual shooting range in my apartment, so why wouldn't you…" He walked to the pole and tested it. Solid. He grinned at her, feeling like a lottery winner. "Will you show me a few things later?"

She smiled, a sweet, shy curve of her lips. "Yes, of course." She pointed down at his belt. "If you'll show me your gun." With a wink, Paige sashayed toward the back of the cottage.

"Fuck," he murmured, watching her sexy ass and

long legs. There was his cock, needin' attention and trying to bust out of his jeans, again. He checked the safety on his Sig and tucked it in his pocket. He glanced around. The little place was neat and clean. Painted white outside and in, she had colorful furniture on light oak floors, and bright paintings on the wall. He followed her down the hall.

His Ranger instincts kicked in and he scouted his surroundings. Flipping on the light in the first room, he saw a big desk with two computers on it and a mess of open books and notepads. The next room, her bedroom, made his breath catch. Her big bed was covered in a white lace quilt and a dozen little colored pillows. A rocking chair stood in one corner, and she'd covered the floor with a mixed pastel rug. Definitely not what he'd expected the bedroom of an exotic dancer to look like. He glanced down the hall where she stood in front of the bathroom sink rinsing her face. She was nothing like he'd expected.

Walking up behind her, he looked at her reflection in the mirror as she took out her contacts. When she turned to him, her face cleared of makeup, he barely recognized her. Young and beautiful with eyes a brilliant shade of blue.

"Wow." Her eyes captured his heart. Clear and honest, sexy and sweet. "Why the dark contacts?"

Rubbing her hands over his chest, she sighed. "When I'm done paying for school and get a job, I want to leave dancing behind. Completely."

"I'd…" He almost asked her to leave it behind right away. But he had no right to make demands. Yet. Maybe after they had spent a few days together… And nights. His hands worked up under her tank top. "I'd like to take that shower now."

She bit her lip and leaned back against the sink. "Do you want to go first?"

He cupped her firm breasts and his cock rammed straight in the air. "We'll go together."

Lifting her arms up over her head, she whispered, "As in, clean? Or dirty?"

Stripping the tank off her body, he stared at her perfect breasts. "Dirty," he croaked and took her nipple into his mouth.

The taste and the heat of her peak on his tongue shot waves of lust rolling through him, hitting him low in the belly. Switching to the other nipple, he flicked it with his tongue, teasing her.

She tunneled her fingers through his hair, holding him tight. "Oh, Slade."

He liked hearing his name in her husky voice. "Paige." He knelt, kissing her belly, burrowing his tongue in her belly button.

"Oh, oh yeah. Please."

He pulled down her shorts, surprised to reveal nothing but a mouthwatering bare pussy. "Do you ever wear underwear?"

She laughed. "Of course I do. But who would I run into at three in the morning on an unmarked dirt road?"

He looked up into her eyes as he licked her mound. Her taste was fresh and sweet.

She shuddered, her lips opening in an "O."

"You might just run into the man who's going to eat you like he was starving." He licked longer, deeper, watching her eyes roll back and close.

"Eat me."

"Oh, darlin'. You're mine." He lapped along the seam of her pussy, watching in amazement as her lips filled and swelled at his touch. "Spread for me."

She set her feet apart and stroked his hair. "I'll do anything for you."

He gave her a wicked grin. "I'll take you up on that later."

A drop of her juices ran down her thigh and he caught it on his tongue. Sweet, like nectar. He moved closer, thrusting his tongue up into her moist folds, licking and kissing her perfect pussy. Easing his mouth up, he lapped toward where her clit stood hard and pointed. Spreading her with his fingers, he sucked her nub.

Her body jerked wildly and small animal squeaks came from her throat.

His balls tightened and his lower back ached for release.

"Close. So close, Slade." Her voice purred from her sexy lips.

He eased his hand down to her slit, paused his

mouth and his hand, then thrust his finger into her opening as he tweaked her clit wildly with his tongue.

"Uh. Uuuh. Oooohhhh!" Her cries echoed around the bathroom as her body rattled to the rhythm of his tongue and finger.

She was tight. His cock needed to feel that snug fit. Damn soon.

She squeaked and purred as she rode out her orgasm, her sheer delight making him nearly as happy as he'd made her.

"Oh, jeez, Slade. You're good." She panted and looked down at him. "So very talented."

He grinned. "Let me show you another trick."

"I have no energy left to—"

He took her clit between his teeth.

She sucked in a breath.

Sliding his middle finger out of her pussy, he slipped it back until it touched her rosebud ass hole.

"You're…yes, right there." She squealed again, her head thrown back and her body quivering.

Nibbling on her clit, he thrust his thumb into her pussy and rubbed her anus with his finger, slippery with her cream. It only took a minute before she popped again.

Deep, aching groans rolled from her as she rode her orgasm, rode his face and his hand.

His gut clenched, his balls cried out for release, his cock dripped pre-cum until the insides of his boxers were wet and sticky.

When she journeyed back to him, he stood and touched the sexy pink blush that spotted her cheeks.

She put her hands on his face. Her lips met his in a joyous passion that speared him down low, clenching his muscles as they fought to hump against her.

"In the shower," he demanded. He untied his boots and slipped them off, unbuckled his belt and hung his pants on a hook.

She opened her medicine cabinet and pulled out a box of condoms. Unopened. "It's been a while." She blushed. "As you could probably tell from my overzealous response."

Tugging her to him, he bumped his hard on against her through his boxers. "You're response was pure heaven for me."

She blinked up at him. "I think that's the nicest thing you've ever said to me."

"Huh?"

She giggled. "Much better than, "You wanna listen, or you want me to stuff you in the trunk?"

He laughed. "We didn't meet under normal circumstances."

"If I hadn't been there myself, I wouldn't believe it."

"Oh, darlin'." His gaze raced over her sweet face. "The stories we have to tell our…" What the hell was he going to say? Kids? Grandkids? Christ, he was moving way too fast.

"Yeah." With her finger, she drew a heart on his chest. "We do have stories."

Their eyes locked in an unexpectedly tender moment. He drifted deep into her blue irises, wondering what she felt. Where they were headed.

When she reached down and grabbed his cock through the cloth, all thoughts flew and primal instinct took over. He pulled her against him, rubbing his shaft against her belly, lifting her so he could do the same thing against her clit.

With a moan, she dropped her head onto his shoulder.

Slade walked backward to the shower, hauling her with him.

She reached down to turn on the water. "Hmmm." She stopped and knelt in front of him, instead.

"Ah, yeah." His shaft filled and pulsed, knowing the pleasure it would have, once her lips got a hold of it.

Locking her eyes onto his, she eased his shorts over his erection and let them drop. Her hand wrapped around his cock, hot and firm. When she looked down, she said, "Oooh. So big."

His belly locked up, ready to pump and shoot his load.

Her pointy little tongue shot out and licked the slit where a drop of pre-cum gleamed. "I want to suck you dry."

"Oh, yeah." He wanted to tell her he'd like that,

but two words were all he could manage with so little blood left in his brain…

Her lips wrapped around his head, hot and soft, her tongue found that spot on the bottom that connected to every nerve in his body. Tickling it, she sent sparks through his flesh.

She took him deep inside her, so fast he nearly lost his balance. Sucking hard, she slowly pulled her mouth back. Then she did it again. A fast thrust in, followed by a lazy withdrawal. This time, her tongue pressed against the vein on the bottom of his staff.

"That's real good, darlin'." He grabbed a hold of the wall to stay upright.

She sucked and licked in the same unbelievable pattern for what felt like forever. His staff filled with more blood, grew and hardened. His skin burned and the base of his spine felt like a hot poker lodged inside him. He was almost there, but didn't want it to end.

Paige's hand brushed across his balls, tickling and cupping. He almost lost it. Her knuckles flattened against the skin just behind his sack, pressing upward in massaging pulses. He nearly shot into her. Her hand moved back further, his mouth opened on a silent scream.

She wouldn't…

She did. Pressing a finger to his ass hole, she made one circle around it.

He came. His roar of pleasure accompanied the

blast furnace in his head. He grabbed her hair and pumped into her. Red-hot lights flashed behind his eyelids and waves of intense combustion raced through his bloodstream, jolting his arms and legs, tightening his torso. Long pumps of his balls shot everything he had deep down her throat.

She moaned, her throat closing around him as she swallowed, sucked, swallowed more.

Slowly the flames receded, leaving him toasted like a marshmallow on a stick. "Darlin', you did what you promised." He opened his eyes. "I'm sucked dry."

Her blue gaze watched him as she eased her mouth from him. "I had to go deep to get you off. You've got a lot of stamina." She encircled the base of his cock with her finger and thumb and squeezed them to the head. A squirt of cum oozed out and she lapped it up. "And you taste fantastic."

His hand on her hair tightened. "Paige." He wanted to tell her she was everything. What he'd been looking for in a woman. *More* than what he'd ever hoped to find. He pulled her to her feet. Kissing her, he tasted himself in her mouth. He'd never done that before, but he needed to connect with her, bond with her. Make love to her. He stepped back and smiled. Make love.

Turning on the water, he drew back the curtain. "Shower with me?"

She smiled. "Absolutely."

They stepped in, cozying themselves in the

steamy shower. He washed her hair, taking time to lather it thoroughly, twice. Long and thick, he rubbed in her coconut conditioner, combing it through with his fingers.

"My turn." She washed his hair and used shampoo on his chest hair.

He soaped her body first, every inch, then used the handheld shower spray to rinse her, teasing her nipples to peaks, pulsing warm water onto her clit and her pussy lips. "Turn around."

She did, standing with her feet spread, her hands on the wall. With her back to him, she tipped her sweet ass up in the air so he could shoot a soft pulse of water onto her rosebud anal opening. She moaned.

His cock jumped to attention. He could almost feel himself slipping inside her tight pussy, thrusting inside from behind. Stepping one foot out, he grabbed the box of condoms. Variety pack. He ripped it open and pulled out an extra large. Stepping back in, his gaze locked with hers. She had a bar of soap in her hands and had made a huge pile of suds. "Turn around."

Not sure what she had in mind, he turned his back to her. Starting at his shoulders, she rubbed the suds over his skin with deep massaging circles.

"God, that feels good."

"It's just the first course."

"Mmmm." He could get used to being spoiled this way. His life as a Ranger meant very little down time.

He had an apartment in Amarillo that he hadn't seen in six weeks.

When she'd thoroughly soaped his back and butt, she used some kind of scrubber, softly circling it over his back, down his ass, then over his arms.

It felt like heaven. The intense sensations on his skin did strange things to his cock and balls, made him crazy to bury himself in her tight pussy. He turned around, his cock stood hard and hot.

She glanced down at it then back at him with a naughty grin. "I guess you like that?"

"Guess I do." He reached for her, but she held out a hand.

"Let me hose you off."

He turned his back to her and let her use the handheld spray to take off the lather. The pulsing pattern of the water relaxed his muscles even more. She concentrated it on his butt, then turned down the water pressure and aimed it between his ass cheeks as he'd done to her. The contact shot his lust into orbit.

He used a hand towel to dry off his cock. "Are you wet?"

She moaned. "How do you mean wet?"

He ripped open the condom packet.

"Is your pussy dripping juices for me?"

"Oh, yeah. I'm slick for you. Wet and hot and tight." She circled her finger over his anus.

The combination of the hot, pulsing water and her talented finger nearly popped him off. He rolled on the condom and turned around, grabbing her, knocking the hose from her hand.

She held onto his shoulders. "Wow, I guess I found your hot spot."

He pressed her up against the tile wall. "I've got a dozen hot spots, darlin'. I expect you'll find each one."

Wrapping her arms around her neck, she kissed him. "My pleasure," she whispered against his mouth.

"Now, it's my pleasure." Slade reached down and grasped her knees. Pulling her legs up, he opened her wide for him. Looking deep into her beautiful blue eyes, he slid his cock into her cunt.

Her eyes rolled back and her mouth dropped open with a joyful squeal. Her body shook and her fingernails dug into his back. "Fuck me hard, Ranger."

His balls shuddered as his cock jerked inside her. He pulled out and slammed back in. "Too much?" he murmured, waiting for her body to stretch and fit him inside.

"Not enough. Do me fast."

Gritting his teeth to keep from blowing too early, he pumped into her, her snug slit fitting around him like a fist. "God, you're tight."

"I'm so full. Your cock is so damn big." She tilted her hips and her back made slurpy sounds against the wet shower wall. Her hands ran over his shoulders, down his arms that flexed tight to hold her where he wanted her.

He pulled her closer, pushed his cock even deeper inside her, thrusting rabidly, taking and giving everything. Her breasts bounced with the movement, raking her diamond-hard nipples over his pecs. Lightning bolts of desire raced up and down his spine. Twinges of orgasmic shocks flashed in his mind as pulses of electricity shimmered through his cock and balls.

Paige's cries took on a wild tone. She was close.

He bent his head and took her earlobe into his mouth, biting and sucking, wanting to get her off, but not able to use his hands. His kisses found a sweet spot on her neck. Her clean taste and smooth skin caused his hips to work faster, propelling him toward release.

She shouted as his mouth ravaged her.

He lifted his head. "Touch your clit for me, darlin'."

"Slade." Her eyes locked with his. She licked her middle finger and slid it between their bodies. Pressed against his pubic bone, she let him do the work of sliding her finger up and down on her clit.

He pistoned into her, their breaths chugging in and out, their gazes melding. He felt it build and couldn't stop it. "I'm…gonna…come."

She howled as her body tightened and shimmied with orgasm.

He let loose, pumping his cum into her. His mind seized with ecstasy. His heart walloped in his chest, sending blood racing through his veins. Every inch of his skin tingled. He thrust mindlessly, his balls empty but his cock still hard and sensitive. A final shudder brought him back around to reality and he opened his eyes.

She hung in his arms, breathless, boneless, and smiling so beautifully, he wished he could take a picture.

"You're sexy when you come."

She sighed. "You're sexy when you make me come." She grabbed fistfuls of his hair. "Mmm. You're outrageous. Do you know that?"

Outrageously infatuated. "You're perfect for me, Paige." It was the closest he'd ever come to saying those life-changing three little words.

"Ohhh," she sighed, her smile sappy-sweet, and pressed her lips to his.

He kissed her gently, reveling in the afterglow that swirled around them like steam from the hot shower. He could get used to this.

He set her on her feet and they rinsed off again. Stepping out, he used a big, fluffy University of Texas at Austin towel, to wrap her like a mummy.

Smiling up at him, she used a corner of the towel to dry his chest and shoulders. "How did you get involved in the cattle rustling thing?

Slade grabbed another towel and dried her hair. "I'm part of the organized crime operation."

"Really? The mafia is stealing cows?"

He grinned. "More or less."

"So, what's going to happen to those men you were with?" She picked up her hairbrush.

He held out his hand. She gave him the brush and he turned her to face the mirror, starting on the snarls at the ends. "I planted a tracking device on the truck. They've got a two-day drive to wherever they go to drop off the load."

"Can't they just arrest them now?"

"They want the big guys." He finished with her hair and ran the brush through his own. He liked the domestic feel of sharing personal items.

Her blue eyes watched him in the mirror. "Slade?"

"Mm hm?" He wrapped his arms around her, pressing her back to his chest. Warm and soft and curvy. Cute and funny and brave. She was a keeper.

"Are you from around here?"

"Amarillo. I'm with Rangers Company C in Lubbock."

"Since you're so far from home, would you like to stay the night?" Her gaze flicked down, then caught his eyes in the mirror again. "I mean, it's almost morning…"

"I guess I didn't tell you. You're stuck with me for three days."

Her eyes went wide. "Really?"

"Until they have those men in custody, I need to stay close to you."

"You're here to protect me?" Her smile slid warm

and inviting across her lips. "I like that."

He turned her around and tugged her flush against him. "Yeah. Between lookin' at my gun, and puttin' that pole in the living room to use, we should have us a good time."

"We will." She ran her fingers through his chest hair.

He stroked her damp hair.

"Then you're going back to Lubbock?" Her voice sounded unconcerned, but he saw the intensity in her eyes. His answer meant a lot to her.

"I have to, but I've been thinking about a transfer." He'd started thinking about it today. When he met Paige.

She grinned up at him, her face lit with expectation. "There's an office here in Austin."

His heart thumped. She wanted him close? He could ask to work with Company H—he looked into her eyes—if things worked out as well as he imagined they would in the next three days. "It's a possibility."

"Damn. I sounded pushy, didn't I." Her smile wavered. "We've only known each other for a short time." She dropped her head.

Crooking a finger under her chin, he lifted her head until their gazes met. "You've got something special."

"Besides the dumb blonde thing?"

He brushed his thumb over her bottom lip. "Paige. I've never been this crazy for any other woman."

Her eyes filled with emotion. "I'm feeling it, too." After a long moment, she sighed. "I'm so glad you didn't kill me."

He laughed. "I'm glad you *did* kiss me."

~ ~ ~ ~

No Way Out

Holter Ford removed his cowboy hat as he approached the bank president's administrative assistant. "Afternoon, Betsy."

Sitting at her desk with her eyes glued to her computer monitor, she smiled up at him. "Good afternoon, Sheriff." Gesturing behind her to the open door marked "President," she winked. "Go on in. Alissa's expecting you."

He nodded and walked across the brown industrial carpet and stopped at the threshold.

Alissa Voigt, bank president since her parents retired to Florida five years ago, sat behind her big cherry wood desk. Her leather chair was turned sideways to him and she faced the window to the street. She stared out, chewing on the tip of her pen, her kissable red lips caught his attention.

As always when he saw her, his gut did a hungry roll. Today, she'd pulled her auburn hair into a twist at the back. Her tall, thin body was covered by one of her dark, all-business suits, but a pale green blouse peeked out of the jacket.

"Ms. Voigt?"

She jumped and raised a hand in a defensive stance. Odd, he'd never seen her anything but confident and friendly. She exhaled a choppy breath and set down her pen. "Sheriff." She stood. "Thanks for coming." She extended her hand.

He walked across the office and shook her hand over her desk. The touch of her cool palm raised a wicked spark across the hair on his bare forearm.

Her blue eyes locked with his for a second before skittering away. "Please have a seat." Gesturing to the leather chairs in front of her desk, she stepped out from behind it and strode to the door. Her skirt ended a couple inches above her knees and her perfect calves stretched down long and trim, ending at her high-heeled pumps.

His fingers tingled, wanting to caress those legs, fling off the sexy shoes, and stroke from her feet clear up to…

Alissa closed the door and turned to him.

His gaze shot quickly from her calves to her face.

A brief, knowing smile curved her lips. "Of course you won't sit until I do, right Sheriff?" Her gaze flicked up toward his forehead, then away.

He ran quick fingers through his short, blond hair, freeing it from its hat-hair flatness.

She walked to the mini-fridge tucked into a cabinet on the other side of the small conference table. "Would you like some water? It's hot out there today."

Hot in here, too. Or was it just her? He hadn't been in her office since three years ago when he moved to town to take the sheriff's job. Then, he'd come to her for a loan to buy his ranch on the outskirts of town. Newly divorced and dried up on life, he'd soaked up her kindness and concern. She'd been completely professional back then, exactly what he'd needed to help get his life back on track. But now, he needed more. Felt more. She'd been on his mind a lot lately.

As she bent over to retrieve a bottle, her skirt snugged around her tight, round ass.

"Yes," he said. It came out a growl.

She straightened and looked at him wide eyed.

He cleared his throat. "I'd appreciate a water, ma'am."

She stepped to his side and handed him the bottle. "Please, call me Alissa." In her heels, she stood at eye-level. Her gray eyes were surrounded by long, dark lashes that fluttered attractively on her pale skin. "'Ma'am' makes me feel too old." Her scent, like roses and rainwater, found its way into his nostrils and gave his head a spin.

He knew from the high school yearbooks in the town library that she was thirty-five. A few years older than him. She looked a lot younger than him, though. He'd lived a tough life as a lawman in Bozeman. He purely loved being a small-town sheriff.

"You'll call me Holt, then." They'd attended a great many town functions, but never together. They'd flirted, bought each other drinks, done a lot of chatting close-up, but he'd never asked her out.

Rumor had it she didn't date anyone in town.

She surprised him by perching on the edge of the guest chair next to his.

He folded his lanky frame into his chair and laid his hat on the corner of her desk.

Reaching under her desk calendar, she pulled out a folded piece of paper. "This was left on my car in the back parking lot." She handed it to him and he took it carefully by the edges. "The security guard saw it this afternoon and brought it in to me."

Alissa Voigt was scribbled on the front. Opening it, he read the scrawled words. *You took everything from me. Now I'm gonna take everything from you.*

Holt read it once more and looked at her.

Her hands were clasped together in her lap. Her face showed worry.

"Any idea what this means? Who it's from?"

She shook her head. "Things are difficult right now. People are losing their homes, their businesses." With a sigh she slid back in her chair. "We've had to foreclose and repossess a few places." Her eyes flashed sorrow. "But only as a last resort."

He knew that was true. One of his deputies' wives was going through cancer treatment. They and their four kids had been on the verge of losing their home. Alissa worked some kind of miracle to keep them from going under, and things were better for them now, financially and health-wise.

"Security cameras?"

She shook her head. "Not pointed in that direction."

"Is this the first note you've received like this?"

She glanced down and shook her head. "I received another one yesterday." Her gaze met his. "At home."

"Do you still have it?"

"No. I put it out with the trash. I didn't think it was serious." Her voice grew quiet.

He fought the urge to haul her into his arms and tell her he'd take care of this. Take care of her, no matter what. "Did it say the same thing?" He set the letter on the desk.

"No. It said, 'Why did you have to do it? I've lost everything, now'."

"Lost. Everything. Now," he murmured. He rubbed his beard stubble and tried to recall townsfolk who had lost more than just property.

She sat forward. "I was just going through the list of foreclosures over the last three months." She stood and walked behind her desk. "Would you like a printout?"

He stood automatically when Alissa did, as his mama had taught him. "Let's go through it together."

Her surprise showed in her eyes. "Okay." She checked her watch.

"Do you have somewhere to be tonight? A date?" He gave himself a mental headslap. Where the hell had that come from?

Alissa's brow furrowed. "No. I don't have a date."

She looked at him strangely, then her eyes twinkled and her lips thinned as if she were biting back a grin. "The bank is closing in a few minutes and I want to be sure everything's tucked in for the night."

He nodded, feeling like an ass. "Right." He patted his pocket for his phone. "I'll report in to my deputies. With your approval, I'll have one of them pick through your garbage for that note."

She grimaced. "Lucky guy. Sure, he's welcome to dig through it. The container is just inside the garage door. It's unlocked."

He clamped his jaw tight. A beautiful woman, living alone, leaving her doors unlocked.

"I know what you're thinking." Walking out from behind her desk, she stopped in front of him. "But this is Tuckers Bend, for heaven sakes."

Holt flicked the corner of the threatening note on her desk. "Times are changing."

Her gaze dropped to the paper then came back up to meet his. She crossed her arms over her stomach and glanced out the window. Clouds had moved in and rogue gusts of wind carried the first raindrops of a promised storm. "I guess so." Her voice choked as a shiver rattled through her.

Before he could stop himself, he wrapped his hand around her arm. "I'm here, Alissa. I'll do everything in my power to keep you safe."

The look she gave him would have invoked the superhero in any man. Trust, innocence, hope, all combined in one beautiful pair of eyes.

Not knowing who moved first, he put his other hand on her back as she wrapped her arms around his waist.

With his lips just inches from hers, rockets fired from his brain, lodging themselves deep down in his belly, turning everything hard and unsettled.

"Thank you, Holt." She made the move, lifting her lips to his and brushing softly.

He took it to the next level, needing to taste her. His tongue slid past her lips, caught on her teeth, then tangled with hers in a kiss so hot, he lost awareness of his surroundings.

Her response was immediate. Her hands fisted on the back of his uniform shirt, her small cry filled the air between them.

Holt slowed the kiss, running his hand up and down her long spine. When he pulled back an inch, he stared into eyes that turned dark and droopy-lidded with passion. Her parted lips tempted him to go in for more. Much more.

Alissa closed her perfect mouth and swallowed. "I've been wondering what that would feel like," she whispered.

Her admission shook him like an earthquake. Besides long, questioning glances during their conversations, and a double-meaning suggestion now and then, she'd never given him a sign.

He brushed his thumb over her full lower lip. "I've

been wondering the same."

Her lips curved up. "Yet you never asked me out?"

Taking her hands in his, he shrugged. "I heard you didn't date town folk."

She nodded. "As a rule." Gesturing toward her closed door, she said, "Sooner or later everyone in town comes through that door, and it's best to keep business and pleasure separate." She eased her hands out of his. "Which reminds me." She walked to the door. "I need to check on a few things."

"Wait." He held up his hand. "So why break your dating rule today?"

Her smile flashed bright. "Do you believe in fate, Sheriff Ford?" She turned the handle and opened the door. "I do."

She left the door open and he watched her walk away. Her hips swung just enough to do rowdy things to his private parts. Walking to the threshold, he pulled out his phone and gave his deputies directions. He kept an eye on Alissa as she double-checked that the front doors were locked securely. She verified the safe was closed and locked, then said goodnight to her staff and ensured the back doors locked after them.

After flipping the main lights off, she turned toward him. Their gazes met across the dimly lit room. A flash blasted outside the windows and Holt's right hand dropped to the grip of the Smith & Wesson holstered at his side. The crack of thunder relieved his initial adrenalin rush.

Light footsteps drew closer. "Looks like we're in for a wild night."

"Yep." Breathing deep, he smelled her rosy scent. Every nerve in his body told him to pull her close and show her what a wild night he had in mind, but that would have to wait. "Should we get to that list?"

"Yes." She walked into her office and unhooked her laptop from its docking station. "Let's sit at the conference table."

He grabbed his water and took a seat facing the door and the window. His years in law enforcement had taught him to treat every situation as if it were critical. To observe everything with an eye toward safety. After five years, it had driven his ex-wife crazy. Driven her right out of his life. That had been three years ago. He'd been alone since then. How would Alissa feel about dating a lawman?

She carried her laptop and two notepads to the table. Sitting on the chair next to his, she crossed her legs.

He couldn't help but stare at the sexy curves and temptingly flawless skin.

"Sheriff?" When their eyes met, she gave him a seductive smile. "Ready?"

Oh hell yeah, he was ready. His cock was on high alert and he leaned forward to cover the evidence of his lust. "Let's start with the most recent and work backward."

For the next hour and a half, it was all business. They went through her records and listed names and pertinent information on their tablets. Holt contributed what he knew about criminal charges, auto and livestock repossessions, and divorces. They had a list of a half-dozen possibilities and three strong suspects.

At around seven thirty, his stomach rumbled so loudly, Alissa started. "You must be starving." She stood and went to the small refrigerator and did that sexy bending-over trick that turned his mind to mush.

"I'm fine. We won't be here too much longer."

She pulled out two takeout containers. "Might as well eat these up." She set them on the table and opened the first box. A salad with tomatoes and strips of salmon gave off the pungent scent of Italian dressing. The second held a huge hamburger in a bun surrounded by French fries. She grinned. "Which looks good to you?"

He raised a brow.

She laughed and stuck the entire burger box in the little microwave and got it spinning. "Would you like a Coke?"

"Sounds good."

She pulled out a regular and a diet, set napkins and silverware on the table, and pushed aside her laptop.

"You eat in here a lot?" He opened the Coke and

drank. The cold carbonation refreshed him after a brutal evening trying to keep his mind off that kiss—and what would come next.

"It's easier to work straight through lunch and get home at a decent hour." She pointed to the salad. "This was today's lunch." She gestured to the microwave. "That was last night's dinner. I hope it tastes okay."

He gave a humorless laugh. "I'm a bachelor. I'll eat just about anything."

Their eyes locked for a moment, and a pink blush colored her cheeks. Was she thinking the same thing he was? He'd lift that tight skirt up over her thighs, tug aside her panties. Lay her out on the table and lick her pussy until she came like thunder.

The microwave beeped. She blinked a couple times then turned. Retrieving his meal, she set the container in front of him with a bottle of ketchup. After removing her jacket, she perched on the chair next to his and picked at the lettuce.

The burger tasted pretty good, despite the soggy bun. The limp fries filled his stomach.

Holding the hamburger, he gestured to her box. "Your salad's no good?"

She shrugged and let go of her fork. "Just not hungry." She pulled a face. "This whole threat thing has me rattled."

He nodded. "I don't blame you."

"I'm glad you're here."

A possessive flood of testosterone raced through his bloodstream, but something softer lodged in his chest. He wouldn't be anywhere else.

After a moment, she sniffed the air. "How's your burger? It smells good."

"You need comfort food. Have a bite of this." He held out the burger but she didn't take it, just leaned forward and ate from his hand. Something about the nip of her teeth on his food, the act of feeding her, turned out to be the final piece of the puzzle. He stared at her while she chewed and swallowed, then washed it down with soda. Her graceful neck opened to his lusty gaze. He dropped the burger in his container and stood, pulling her up with him.

Her palms landed on his chest, and through his thin shirt, her heat burned his flesh. Framing her face with his hands, he kissed her. His lips brushed hers then devoured her, unable to wait another minute to feast on her. His tongue slid the length of her velvet one, luring her into his mouth, inviting her to taste him.

His hand went to her hair and without much difficulty, he removed the clip that held her twist. Her soft, shoulder-length hair tumbled down and he ran his fingers through it. His other hand eased down her throat, the back of his fingers brushing her collarbone. The silk of her blouse felt rough compared to her smooth skin and his hand eased lower, sliding inside her blouse to caress the curve of her breast and her silky bra.

Holt lifted his mouth from hers, looking into passion-dark eyes and kiss-swollen lips.

Her fingers trailed to the top button of his shirt. She stopped her movement, suddenly looking uncertain.

"It's happening, Alissa. Keep going." The ache in his belly turned to pure lust, sending blood rushing to his cock.

She unfastened three buttons before his mind clicked back into gear. He grasped the tiny silk button of her blouse in his big fingers and carefully tried to unfasten it. It popped loose and bounced onto the table.

Alissa smiled. "Why don't you finish yours, and I'll—"

A horn blasted twice from the street in front of the building.

She bit her lower lip. "We should close the blinds."

He looked out the window. Although the bank was set back from the sidewalk by a wide patch of grass, people could probably see right in. He kissed her quickly and walked past her desk, pulling out his wallet and removing the condom from it. After he unfurled the horizontal shades, he turned back.

She stood in front of her desk. Looking at his hand, she grinned. "I'm glad you're prepared."

He walked to her, leaned in. "You don't keep a

stock of these in your desk?"

Shaking her head, she propped her butt on the edge. "No. But I will from now on."

The promise in her eyes shook him, melted away his reservations. "I'm putting your office on my list of favorite places to eat."

She reached for him, finished unbuttoning his shirt, and tugged the tails from his waistband. With an appreciative "Mmmm," she slipped her hands over his chest and abs, playing with the light hair across his pecs and tracing it down lower, where it led to his erection.

Her touch pushed him another notch closer to manic.

He pulled her blouse from her shoulders as she stripped his from him. Both their shirts landed in a pile on the floor. He unhooked her green bra easily and took it from her, revealing her small, round breasts tipped with pink peaks.

Her shiver puckered her nipples.

He spanned her waist with his hands then slid them upward, cupping her perfect breasts. "Beautiful. I have to taste you." He tipped his head and took her pebbled peak into his mouth. The taste was like sweet peaches. "I could feast on you for hours."

With a moan, she grabbed his hair, slid her hands down his neck and over his shoulders. "You're all muscle. So strong."

Licking his way to the other breast, he let the

fierce need flow though him. His hips flexed, wanting to pump his shaft inside her, make her his. Circling her with his arms, he lifted her onto the desk.

She leaned back, bracing on her hands. Breathing hard, her hair went wild around her shoulders as she stared at him with wicked desire burning in her eyes.

He couldn't take time for finesse. He tugged her skirt up over her long, trim thighs, until her green panties showed. Too nice to rip off, he grasped them in his fingers and peeled them off her, over her sexy shoes. Holt pressed his palms on her thighs and spread her legs. Her pussy, furred lightly with auburn hair, glistened with her juices.

"God, I want to eat you." Locking his gaze with hers, he bit the tip of his tongue between his teeth.

Her body jittered as if an orgasm overtook her. "No." Her voice cracked and she sucked in a breath. "First, inside me. I want you inside me now." Her eyes showed need and desperation.

His cock pulsed and his balls tightened, his body rippling with heat. Unfastening his holster, he set his gun on the chair behind him. After toeing off his boots, his pants and briefs followed and he turned back to her.

"You are magnificent, Holt." Her eyes roamed over his body. "I've dreamt of this. Of you."

Her admission had him thinking back to all the nights he'd imagined her in his bed. "You've been my fantasy, Alissa." His staff jerked, filling with blood, pulsing with the acute need to fuck her. Taking a breath to hold himself back from ravaging her, he opened the condom packet and rolled it on. He pulled her to the edge of the desk and lifted her legs. He slid one shoe off her foot and kissed her arch.

She sighed and dropped her head back, giving him a sensual view of her neck.

He removed her other shoe and nibbled on her toe.

Alissa moaned, her body shook with a shiver that raised bumps on her skin.

Unable to wait another second, his fingers brushed her mound.

She jerked her head up with a sweet little cry.

The musky scent of her pussy raced into his brain and drove him nearly frantic.

Slowing his breath, he focused on her eyes as he stroked her, petting her soft, swollen lips. He explored her hidden clit, watching her face turn desperate and hungry. Sliding a finger into her wet slit, he groaned as her tight opening contracted around him.

"You're wet, Alissa. You're ready for me."

"Yes." Biting her bottom lip, she snuck a foot around his back and pulled him closer.

His cock bobbed at the entrance to her core. He lifted her long legs onto his chest, her feet at his ears, the touch of her satiny flesh on his body shooting spears of desire to his balls.

She leaned back further, propped up on her elbows, her lungs pumping in air, her face flushed with a sexy pink.

Spreading his legs, he found the perfect angle and touched his throbbing head to her slit.

Her needy cry turned stormy as he slid his staff into her dripping cunt.

Holding her hips to press himself deeper into her, he called, "Alissa." Everything inside him ached for release, fought to surrender to the ecstasy and empty into her.

Her slit tightened around him and she circled her hips.

He pulled out of her and looked down at his cock, dripping wet with her juices. The cool air gripped him, providing the moment of control he needed. He plunged back into her, starting his collapse all over again.

He pulled back, slid into her, each thrust building the tension in his spine, pushing the moment of release closer and closer to his brain.

She rolled her head on her neck, her tiny puffs of breath matching the soul-searing thrusts of his cock. When her cries turned critical, he reached for her clit.

Focusing on her pleasure, he pistoned into her, matching the motion of his thumb on her clit. Within seconds, she stiffened and screamed. Her body shuddered as he rode her, flicked her pussy.

He followed her down. The blast from his balls hit

him so hard, he cursed—something he never did during sex. Her cunt tightened with her orgasm, gripping his cock so fiercely, he felt a second roll of orgasm shake through him. Lightning flashed behind his eyelids and rattled down his spine, zinging through his body in shock waves of electricity.

The heat, the incredible bliss passed slowly, bringing him back to reality with a soft smile. "Holy shit."

She chuckled. "I'm thinking that exact same thing." Her eyes were dark, her cheeks, neck and chest a gorgeous pink as her lungs pumped in oxygen. "Holy shit."

Holding the condom, he eased out of her. "I don't want this to end." He meant the sex session, but his heart throbbed an extra beat when he admitted he wanted more of Alissa, too. Holt stroked a hand over her calf and eased her legs down. Picking her up in his arms, he stepped back and sat in her guest chair, holding her against him. The leather felt cool against his heated skin, yet where Alissa pressed against him, he burned with a synergistic fire.

She set her hand on his chest and her head on his shoulder.

He took the plunge. "I'd like to see you. Take you out."

She sighed then lifted her head to look into his eyes. Her sorrowful expression warned him he wasn't going to like this.

His phone rang.

He reached for his uniform slacks and took the phone out of his pocket. "Sheriff."

"Sheriff, it's Dwight." He sounded anxious. "Ms. Voight's house is on fire."

He looked at her and her eyes widened. She crawled off his lap and picked up her blouse, holding it over her breasts.

Holt mouthed, "Bathroom?"

She pointed to a door.

He walked into it and closed the door. "What the hell do you mean, 'on fire'?" Sirens sounded through the phone.

"We were patrolling it, just as you said, and less than a minute ago I drove by and flames were shooting out the front porch windows."

"Shit." He had no clue things would escalate from a couple notes to a firebombing within hours. He should have brought Alissa to the jailhouse. Or hidden her someplace safe. "Lightning?"

"No. It's burning hot. Some kind of accelerant." the deputy shouted over the sirens. "The rain kept it from taking the whole front of the house off."

He dealt with the condom and washed up. "Where's Griff?"

"He's heading your way. I called and told him what was happening here, and he'll be at the bank in a few minutes."

"Okay. You get over here, too. If my guess is

right, the threat is heading here next."

"Will do, Sheriff. Are you gonna get out of there?"

"As soon as Griff gets here, we'll take Ms. Voight's car and use him as an escort out to my ranch."

"They've almost got the fire out. I'm leaving now."

"Call me when you're here." He hung up and stepped out of the bathroom.

The lights were off and her office door stood open a few inches. "Alissa?"

"Over here." Her voice came from near the door. "What's going on?"

He crossed to his clothes and pulled on his briefs. "Your house was on fire."

She huffed in a breath.

"They caught it quickly, just the front porch sustained damage." He pulled on his shirt, stepped into his pants and boots, fastened his gun at his hip, and went to Alissa.

She was shaking when he took her into his arms. "What are we going to do?"

"One of my deputies should be here any—"

A loud blast from the back of the bank made them both jump.

"Damn it." He knew that sound.

"What is it?" she cried.

"I'm guessing…your car."

His phone rang. He saw Griff's number. "What the hell is going on?"

"Her car. The gas tank exploded. I saw the flames and called the fire department just before I called you."

Holt looked down. In the dim light coming from the banking area, her eyes showed panic.

"Your car, honey," he said quietly.

"Um…" Griff said. "And your truck. The flames are doing a number on your paint job."

He couldn't work up any worry about his truck. Everything focused on Alissa.

The sound of sirens rang through the phone. "Griff?"

No response except the wail of sirens.

Holt caught a movement through the glass doors facing the street. A car. With no lights on. "Griff, get to the front of the building!" He didn't know if the deputy heard him.

Adrenalin pumped as he tugged Alissa with him toward the back of her office. "Get in the bathroom. Stay there."

"No. I can—"

Pushing her into the room, he looked into her eyes. "He's here." He closed the door as her hands went to her mouth and her eyes flashed wildly.

As he stepped away, he heard her voice. "Be careful, Holt. Please."

Her words swelled a yearning in his chest. It'd

been a long time since anyone cared enough to worry about him.

Easing his gun out of its holster, he peered out the door. The car hadn't stopped at the front doors. A sick feeling clutched his gut. He ran to Alissa's office window and looked out through the slits. The rain pouring down the window made everything murky, but he knew the shadow of a man. And it was walking right toward him.

Holt tugged the shade, ripping it from the window. Using a chair, he broke the glass. Half the pane shattered, raining down and cutting his hand. He drew his weapon.

The bank's alarm system immediately starting whirring.

The figure stopped about ten feet away, and a flame caught quick and bright. He pulled his arm back as if to throw.

"Drop it or I'll shoot."

The figure froze for a second, then shouted, "Go to hell!"

All the training and practice of a lifetime couldn't stop the gut-deep ache of having to shoot a person. Holt aimed for his shoulder and squeezed the trigger.

The man jerked back, dropping the flaming device. It didn't break as Holt expected. The perp turned and leaned down to pick it up with his other hand.

He aimed for the knee and squeezed off a shot.

The figure pitched sideways and fell flat on his back, groaning with pain.

Holt backed away from the window, expecting the device to explode. He kept his gun trained on the figure on the ground. With the wet grass and the rain, the flame quickly died. The sound of a cruiser siren and red flashing lights raced toward them and screeched to a stop. Dwight jumped out of his patrol car.

Holt pointed his gun toward the ceiling, his gaze never leaving the perp.

Griff pulled up from the other direction. In seconds, they had the man cuffed and Mirandized.

Dwight walked up to the window. "Everything okay in there?"

Holt flicked on the safety and lowered his gun. "We're good." He nodded toward the man in the back seat of Griff's cruiser. "Who is it?"

"Baylen Fry."

He was one of the three men Alissa and he had circled as likely suspects.

"Baylen did this?" Alissa's voice came from directly behind him. "I can't believe it."

He turned and saw her barefoot, a button missing on her blouse, her hair rumpled and sexy.

"He's been out of control since his wife left and took their kids," Holt said.

Dwight nodded. "We'll get him locked up then I'll come back."

"Thank you, Deputy," she told Dwight. "I appreciate your being here, and at my home."

He tipped his hat. "My pleasure, ma'am. I'm glad you're safe."

"We'll get the alarm shut off and open the front door." Holt looked at Alissa. "I'll call Sam from the lumberyard and have him cover up this window and the ones at your house."

"Uh, boss?" Dwight's brows furrowed.

He looked at his deputy. "Yeah?"

"You might want to button your shirt first." Dwight looked past him and tipped his hat. "Ma'am." He grinned and walked away.

"Shit." Holt looked down at his bare chest.

"It's not that bad, is it?" She looked up at him with a watery smile.

He recalled her hesitancy earlier when he'd asked her if she'd date him. "I'll talk to him. Tell him we don't want this spread all over town." He set his gun down and started buttoning his shirt. His fingers shook as the adrenaline of the past few minutes flowed out of him.

"Holt." Her voice was sweet. "I *do* want this spread all over town. When you asked me earlier if we could go out?"

His hands froze on the second button.

She stepped closer and worked on the third. "I wanted to warn you that it's going to be a lot faster and a lot hotter than just dating." She finished and slid her hands up his chest.

He felt them shake and pulled her tight against him. "Honey, are you okay?"

She tucked her face into his neck and a sob left her throat. "I was so afraid for you, Holt."

"Aw, Alissa." His chest constricted. "I promised I'd do everything I could to keep you safe."

"You risked your life for me." She looked up at him, her beautiful blue eyes wet, tears streaking down her face.

"I'd do it again. In an instant." It was his job. His belly clenched. "Now that you've seen what I deal with, can you handle sharing your life with a lawman?"

She smiled through her tears and nodded. "There's no one in the world I'd like to be with, besides you." She sucked in an uneven breath. "Remember, Sheriff Ford? I believe in fate."

His body heated with an emotion he couldn't name. All he knew was, he never wanted to let her go. He kissed her, showing her without words how desperately he needed her. Kissing a path to her ear, he whispered, "You've made a believer out of me, Ms. Voight."

~~~~
~~~~

Private Lessons

Tabatha Griggs pulled her little VW Beetle into the parking spot next to the only other vehicle in the lot, a big, shiny red pickup truck. The brand new Ford belonged to *him*, Rance O'Hanlon. Local boy turned pro bull rider—whom she'd had a crush on since seventh grade.

The front of the Two-Step Saloon looked drab in the afternoon light, no neon signs flashing, no tracer lights circling the door. Straightening her broomstick skirt, she wished, once again, she hadn't let her friends help her dress. The skirt ended at the top of her cowgirl boots, and her halter top clung to her braless breasts. She looked ready for a night on the town, not an afternoon on a mechanical bull.

Her left hand clutched the Bull Riding Lesson certificate her girlfriends won in a silent auction benefiting the local food pantry. The sneaky bitches had listed her name as the winner, and now, here she was, ten minutes late for her lesson because those same rotten friends kicked her out of the apartment they shared—before she could put on underwear.

Taking deep breaths, she marched to the front door and opened it. In the middle of the room, Rance rode the bull at full speed, his shirt open, Stetson pulled down tight, and his right arm whipping the airspace above his head.

She'd seen him ride plenty on TV, and a couple times in person. But the live version of the man was as big and bold as all Texas. Had she ever seen anything that gorgeous?

The ride ended and she murmured, “Wow.”

He heard her. As he turned toward her, a beam of light caught him. His smile sent the floor under her feet rattling. Or was that just her body quivering?

Jumping down from the bull, he called, “Didn’t think you were going to show up, Miss Tabatha.” He walked toward her and took her hand. “I’m real glad to see you.” Rance stared into her eyes, the focus in his ocean-blue irises startled her.

A tingling worked its way from her hand up to her chest. Normal breathing became nearly impossible.

Had she ever been this close to him? She'd worshiped him from afar, but worshiping him from up close was so much better.

“C’mon,” he said tugging her gently into the padded ring, moving his hand to her elbow to steady her.

His touch on her arm grew bolder and his fingers brushed along the swell of her breast. Lightning bolts shot through her nerve endings, ending low in her belly and causing sweetly painful contractions to vibrate in her core.

When she looked up at him, his sideling glance held a good measure of wicked.

He patted the mechanical bull. “Hop on.”

Thinking of the way the bull had whipped him around, her nerves wrangled her mind into a slight panic. "Rance, I'm not sure about this."

"Sorry, no refunds." He chuckled and moved closer. "You'll be fine. We'll go easy, and I'll be right next to you the whole time." His hands spanned her waist.

His touch, hot and firm through her slinky top, made her mouth water with anticipation. Would he kiss her?

He bent closer, and without warning lifted her onto the bull.

She let out a squeaky cry as he plopped her sideways on the slick leather.

"Unless you wanna ride sidesaddle..." His wink teased her. "Swing your leg over."

She had to hike up her skirt to get her leg over the saddle horn.

He stood close, boldly scanning her calf, her knee, then her thigh. "Nice," he murmured and gave her a smile that heated her blood and tingled into her nipples, tightening them into needy, painful points.

He noticed them, too. The promise of pleasure in his gaze made her catch her breath as her pussy flooded with moisture.

He spent a few moments adjusting something under the bull then working the controls at the booth. "Ready?" he called.

"No." She gripped the horn tightly, suddenly more

nervous about the bull ride that the bull rider.

He laughed. “Easy there, cowgirl. It’s on the lowest setting. It's like the kiddy rides at the fair.”

Yeah, if the fair was held during a tornado. Swallowing her fear, she croaked, "Okay. Ready."

The bull began to move, a slow, mesmerizing rhythm that swiveled her hips. Through her skirt, her pussy lips rubbed against the vibrating leather. Mmm, this wasn't so bad. Actually, it was very nice. She needed one of these in her apartment.

“Relax into it,” his voice rumbled, low and sexy. “Try holding on with just one hand.”

She went from a two-handed death-grip to a one-handed. When she felt herself slide, she grabbed a hold again. “I don’t think I can.”

Rance jumped up behind her, startling her. Sliding his body close, he pressed up tight against her back. Oh, heavens, that hard, naked chest tight against her bare upper back set flashes of delight to her breasts and slit.

“Tabatha,” he whispered, hot in her ear. “I was so damn excited when I saw your name listed as the winner.”

Coherent thought eluded her for a moment, but she came up with, “It was nice of you to donate this lesson to benefit…” As his hands wrapped around her waist, her words scattered like dry leaves in the hot, Texas wind. His big, rough hands eased under her top and brushed the sensitive skin on her stomach.

"You know, sugar," he murmured, his lips tickling her ear. "I've had a thing for you since high school."

"You did?" She tipped her head, giving him better access to her neck. "Why didn't you…"

He growled and pressed hot kisses to her earlobe, trailing his mouth down her neck, nipping and tasting with the tip of his tongue. Their bodies writhed together to the hypnotic rhythm of the bull, taunting both of them with the seductive movement.

"You were so cute, with your braces and thick glasses. But we ran in different circles." He pulled her closer. Against her butt she felt his hard cock, hot, even through layers of clothes. "I was a poor ranch hand's son. You were the mayor's daughter."

The thought of him wanting her all those years ago gave her heart a squeeze.

"I couldn't have you then, but I want you now." His voice sounded rough and demanding. Her pussy flooded, swelling her lips and sending hot flushes of lust deep into her belly.

"Take me," she pleaded, leaving behind any sense of modesty. She wanted him. Reaching back between their bodies, she found his immense, hard length beneath his zipper. She stroked and squeezed.

His body shook as a feral groan rumbled out of his chest. Moving his hands slowly, tauntingly upward, he cupped her breasts. "So perfect, Tabatha." His thumbs stroked her nipples, his touch on her intensely sensitive buds shot piercing arrows straight to her core. Her hips bucked, wanting him fast and wild.

Rance slid his hands down over her thighs and lifted her skirt to bare her legs and her slick, waxed pussy. His hands stopped when he touched her mound. “No underwear?” he breathed against the tingling skin of her shoulder. “You came here looking for a ride, didn’t you.”

His words, his hands on her hot, pulsing pussy lips nearly sent her over the edge. Then he slid one finger up, into the flesh that hid her tiny bud. He stroked her clit, rubbing it side to side, circling, driving her mad. Her mind slid closer and closer to the edge.

His other hand moved between their bodies and she felt him unfasten his belt and unzip his fly. “I want to be inside you when you come.”

“Yes, please, now,” she cried, desperate and insistent.

He freed himself and she heard the snap of latex. Thank heavens he came prepared. Within seconds he lifted her. She scrambled to gather her skirt out of the way. He impaled her, sliding his staff into her wet warmth in one fast, possessive motion.

The feel of his thick cock inside her, stretching her, sent waves of delicious chills through her body. Then he bent her forward. “Move with the bull.” His voice came out choked, dangerous. “Work me,

Tabatha, ride me like mine is the only cock you've ever wanted."

"It is, Rance." The admission flowed from her heart. "I've had a crush on you since seventh grade. You were two years ahead of me, and by the time I got up to high school, you were my fantasy. The bad boy I wanted to let seduce me."

"Aw, sugar. All this wasted time."

"It was worth…" She had to catch her breath as his cock slid all the way out then rammed back in, filling her opening, rattling her mind. "Worth the wait."

"Hang on." He used the remote to speed up the bull's rocking. The increased movement thrust her down onto him harder, and his cock pumped deeper into her, hitting her cervix a couple times in a pleasure-pain jolt that sent her rushing toward nirvana. "Please," she begged, right on the edge.

"Not yet, sugar," he whispered in her ear. "I want this to last a while longer." His hands on her ass kept her moving, kept her in rhythm with his thrusts. Rance bit down on her earlobe, the intensity and surprise of the move swirling wildly through her body, contracting her core and startling her brain toward a soaring climax.

Twisting, she released the saddle horn and pulled his head closer, pressing her lips to his for their first kiss.

Rance felt his hat fly off as Tabatha shoved her

fingers into his hair. He kissed her wildly. The perfect kiss, just as he knew it would be. He'd fantasized about this moment all these years. She tasted sweet, like mint and sugar. Her lips were full and soft. His tongue thrust into her and she responded in perfect synchronization to his cock pumping in and out of her.

He was good enough for her now. His bank account big enough to impress even her father. But all he cared about was Tabatha. Would she be willing to give him a chance? He ended the kiss and she looked at him with her dark green eyes. If he guessed correctly, there was more than just lust there. She wanted him, body…and soul.

When she turned back and grabbed the saddle horn, he reached around and slid a hand between her legs. Feeling her tight slit around his hard shaft as he slid in and out of her, his mind clicked off as insistent bolts of pleasure shot from his balls up his spine. He couldn't wait.

"Come for me. Now," he demanded and moved his thumb to vibrate against her hard clit.

She screamed his name, over and over as her hot pussy creamed onto his fingers. Her slit pulsed and milked his cock. Everything went crazy inside him. His brain spun as explosions of white light flashed behind his closed eyelids and ricocheted through his head.

It felt like he'd never come before, like his balls

had been holding back every other time, waiting for this one moment. This one woman. He poured himself out, shudders racking his skin. The moment expanded into minutes, swamping him with the incredible intensity. Every nerve in his body started pinging then imploding.

Catching his breath, Rance slowed the bull to a crawl and pulled Tabatha back to rest against his chest. Her breath rushed in and out of her lungs, and her skin felt hot. “Thanks,” she puffed out. “For the riding lesson.”

"Did you get your money's worth?" he teased. They rocked together as the bull went into a holding pattern.

"I'm totally satisfied." She sighed. "And I didn't pay a penny. My girlfriends bought it as a surprise for me."

He stiffened and his mind snapped out of his after-sex buzz. "You…didn't buy the lesson."

She turned and looked at him, her brow furrowed. "No. Does that make a difference?"

Hell, yes. He thought she'd spent all that money just to have an hour with him. Thought it'd been her way of making the first move. But it had been a surprise to her. "Shit." He pinched the bridge of his nose. He'd jumped her and taken her from behind like a fucking animal.

She turned sidesaddle, gripping his shoulder. "Rance." She shook him once. "Look at me."

He stared into her beautiful eyes, judging her mood. For a second she looked hesitant, then her jaw set and she heaved in a breath.

"They did it because I've never had the nerve to talk to you." She blurted it all out in a rush. "In school, you were always with a girl. And you'd graduated by the time I got my braces off and started developing…confidence." She grinned.

His gaze flicked down to her perfect breasts. She'd developed, all right. Damn fine, too.

She stared at his chest, looking shy. "When you'd come home from the circuit for holidays, we'd pass on the street. You'd tip your hat but never stopped, never said anything."

His heart double-pumped at her admission. "Here I thought you weren't interested in a dirt-poor rodeo bum."

She paused for a moment. "Do you think I'm that shallow?"

Now it was his turn to hesitate. He'd been poor so long, it'd become a sore spot. "No. Like you said, it's taken me a while to develop…confidence. You've been my fantasy for so many years, I didn't want to mess it up."

A peachy blush rose up her cheeks. "But you never gave me a sign," she breathed.

"This is going to sound pretty stupid." He took a deep breath. "But I was following your lead."

"Jeez, were we dumb." Tabatha shook her head. "I

think we both owe my girlfriends a thank you."

"Yeah." Now that he'd moved back to town, his plan had been to flaunt his wealth, show off a little, let Tabatha see how he'd come up in the world, then ask her out. Her girlfriends had saved him a month of living without her in his life.

He kissed her neck, loving the light sheen of sweat on her skin, tasting her soft, salty flesh. “Lesson’s not over, you know.”

She melted against him and her eyes darkened. He wanted to stare into them the next time they made love, and watch her come. “It’s not?” she asked.

“Next part is at my house.” He wanted to impress her with his fancy new home, but mostly he wanted to get her into his bed.

She smiled, a wicked look that set his cock to hardening again. “You have a bull at your house?”

He nodded. “Yeah, I do, but your next lesson’s going to be a different kind of ride. On my mustache.”

She laughed and ran a finger over the slight bristle of hair on his lip. “It’ll be a wicked ride, cowboy.”

“Sugar, I’ve gotta warn you—you won’t even last eight seconds before you come.” He kissed her, slow and seductive. “Guaranteed. Or your money back.”

~ ~ ~ ~

Stubborn Redhead

Jett McCord sat on the old porch swing looking out over the moonlit fields. His cattle milled around and lowed quietly. The smell of the night-blooming flowers she planted filled the air, reminding him of all he'd lost. In the slough up where the driveway met the road, frogs croaked.

A warm night. His jeans and sleeveless shirt felt too hot. He considered jumping in the pool behind the house. Not much fun alone.

A light went on in the bunkhouse down past the barn. Saturday night. All the ranch hands usually headed to town. Was one of his men feeling as desolate as he was? He ran his fingers down his moustache and over his goatee.

Digging the heel of his boot into the wood floor, he started the swing rocking. Just over two weeks ago, she sat here with him. Talking wedding ideas. Planning how they'd rearrange the living room to make space for her furniture. Mapping out their future.

"Fuck." His life had taken a dive into the manure pile thirteen days ago. He leaned forward, resting his elbows on his thighs. Tunneling his hands into his shaggy red-brown hair, he asked himself—for the six-millionth time—if he should call her. Go to her. Make her listen.

"Aw, hell." She's the one who walked away from him. Told him she needed time to decide if she could ever trust him again. Goddamnit, he hadn't done anything wrong. She'd convicted him on rumors.

So, here he sat, pride intact and righteously indignant. Without the woman he loved.

Stomping his boots on the floor, he leaned back and stretched his arms across the top of the seat. The argument they'd had was epic. Neither of them backing down. Each believing the other was wrong. Maybe he should call her…

Headlights appeared on the road, heading from town. He watched the car speed along for a few minutes, expecting it to pass by the driveway. It turned in. It couldn't be one of his hands returning early. They had their own driveway.

With a lurch of his heart, he recognized the shape of the headlights. A Mustang. It was Penny. His stubborn redhead, Penelope Linder. Thank God she'd come back to him. Or was she just here to pick up her stuff?

He stood and walked to the steps. His pulse raced, chest tightened.

The car door swung open and she stepped out. Damn, she was beautiful. Long, red hair, pale skin, dark blue eyes. Her petite, curvy body in jeans and a t-shirt—a look that made him nuts every time he saw her.

"Jett." Her normally sweet voice sounded raw. As

she walked toward him, light reflected off the streaks of tears running down her face.

"Penny." He swallowed the panic that clawed up from his gut. "Will you come in? Talk to me?" There had to be a way to make her recognize his innocence.

She stopped at the foot of the three steps to the porch.

He held out his hand to draw her up to him.

After a moment's hesitation, she pressed her fingertips onto his palm and drew back.

Her white-gold engagement ring glimmered in his hand.

"No." Everything inside him turned to ice. He stepped down to stand in front of her. Their eyes locked. "Don't give up on us."

Her jaw quivered and her eyes flooded, their beautiful blue glimmering in the moonlight. "I can't trust you any longer."

"I didn't do this, Penny." He wanted to crush her to him until the power of his love made her believe him.

"People saw you together—"

He shook his head. "People saw me walk out of the bar." He glanced away, hating everyone who called Penny to report that her fiancé cheated on her. "They saw her walk out *after* me."

She sucked in an uneven breath. "You walked back in together." A cry left her throat. "Two hours later. You don't deny that."

"All coincidence. I told you everything that morning." He ran his hand over his goatee. His nervous habit when he was frustrated.

Her eyes followed his movement. "I didn't come here to argue. I just wanted to give you back your ring and say goodbye." Her voice turned small and choked.

"Goodbye? Where are you going?" Dread made his voice loud.

She stepped back. "I'm moving to Casper."

"Casper?" That was on the other side of Wyoming. Words of denial froze in his throat.

"I'll stay with Billy and Tara until I find my own place." She backed up another step.

Her brother and his wife. Penny and her mother had been visiting them two weeks ago. That Saturday night, he'd let his friends talk him into going to town to shoot pool and swill beer at the Rusty Spur. His drunk ex-girlfriend, Valerie, walked in and latched on to him. Rubbing against him, trying to kiss him. He'd finally walked out of the bar when she'd gone to the bathroom.

Jett reached his hand to touch Penny. "Baby, don't do this to us."

"Don’t!" She yelled, her face turning red. "Don't call me baby. Not after you slept with another woman."

He dropped his hand. "I explained everything to you. I did not sleep with her." Why wouldn't she believe him? Why did she choose to give credence to what her "friends" saw instead of what he told her?

Hell. He knew why. He tugged at his goatee. Circumstances pointed to his guilt. That night, he'd gotten outside the bar and realized he was too buzzed to drive. He'd taken a walk, ended up in the cemetery, visiting his mother's grave. When he sobered up and hiked back to the Spur, Valerie was sitting in his truck, smoking a cigarette, sipping from a flask.

He'd opened the door and told her to get out, but she wouldn't budge. Short of physically dragging her out, he didn't know how to shake her. He'd grinned at her. "Let's go in and dance." She stumbled out of his truck, they stepped into the bar, and he gave her a five to load the jukebox. When her back was turned, he left. Headed straight home. Went straight to bed. Alone.

Penny's breaths came unevenly. "You smelled of her." Dragging the back of her hand across her cheeks, she wiped away tears. "Cheap perfume and rancid cigarettes."

The memory of that smell still haunted him. Riding home in his truck that night, he had to keep the windows open to handle the stink. In his bedroom, he'd stripped off his clothes and crashed.

Before daybreak that morning, he'd awoken to the stomp of boots in the hallway. Penny walked into his bedroom and flipped on the light.

"Baby," he'd said, rubbing his gritty eyes. "You

came home early."

"What did you do, Jett?" Her desperate voice had stopped him cold.

"What?" His foggy brain couldn't grasp her meaning.

She picked up his shirt from the floor and smelled it. When she looked at the collar, her tears started rolling.

"What is it?" He swung his legs out of the bed and walked over to her in his briefs.

Holding up his shirt, she asked, "Whose lipstick is this?" She thrust it at him, punching his chest.

He looked at the collar. "Aw, shit. Valerie was all over me at the Spur."

She shook her head. "And in your truck?"

His brows furrowed. "She was smoking…"

"I know she was." Throwing a handful of white butts at him, she walked out. He picked up one. It had lipstick on it. The same color that was on his shirt. Hell, there were a dozen. Valerie must have sat in his truck smoking the whole two hours he'd been out walking. Why would she… Had she set this up on purpose?

"Penny, wait. I can explain." He ran after her, catching up to her on the front porch. Grabbing her arm, he spun her around. "I went for a walk and she—"

"I know what she did." Penny yanked her arm out of his grasp. "I know what you did." A sob staggered her. "I got four calls in the middle of the night telling me you left the Spur with Valerie not far behind. Hours later, you walked back in together." Her hand curled into a fist. "You didn't even try to hide it."

"No. Nothing happened." Shit. His frustration level built as the evidence piled up to bury him.

"Oh, God, Jett." Her face paled then turned bright red. "Did you do this on purpose? You wanted me to find out?" Her hand went to her heart. "Did you want to break up with me?"

Panic had seized him. "No!" From deep inside, he'd started to shake. "I love you. I'd never cheat on you. Hear me out."

He'd told her the story of walking to the cemetery, finding Valerie in his truck, hauling her into the bar, then leaving. "Nothing happened. I swear."

Penny had walked to her car, silent.

He'd followed close on her heels. "Don't go. Please."

Opening the car door, she'd mumbled, "I need some time."

"If you love me, stay." He'd held out his hand. "Trust me."

She'd stared at his palm for a long while then dropped her gaze. "I need some time." She'd left.

He'd watched her drive out of his life as the sun rose over the Bridger-Teton National Forest. He figured she'd call later. But one day stretched into two, which stretched into thirteen. He'd lived those days in hell, tortured by his pride and angered by her distrust. Tormented with the knowledge that he should make the first move. But every time he'd reached for the phone or his truck keys, his fucking pride won out.

Now, it was too late. She was leaving him. He held her engagement ring in his hand. The same ring that had made her cry with happiness. It made him want to cry with heartbreak.

In a terible déjà vu of two weeks ago, she walked to her car and he followed.

His brain throbbed as his blood pressure skyrocketed. How could he fix this? What could he do to get her to listen? To believe him?

She opened her car door. The dome light illuminated her back seat full of boxes and suitcases.

She was really doing this. He was losing her.

"Wait." He had to put everything on the line. Haul out the pain he'd packed away last year when his mother died. "Just give me two minutes."

She shook her head and sighed. "There's nothing more—"

"Please." If begging would help, he'd do it. "Don't throw away everything we have—everything we will have for the rest of our lives. Don't end us without hearing me out."

With a nod, she crossed her arms. "All right."

He turned and jogged toward the house, up the stairs, and in the door. At the bookshelf in his office, he searched frantically.

****

Penny watched Jett race into the house. "I should just go," she mumbled. She rubbed her clavicle. Her heart was physically sore from the stress and crying jags of the last two weeks.

Heavens, was it only fourteen days ago? It felt like a year. The phone calls from friends that horrible night, the race back from Casper. Walking into Jett's bedroom expecting to see that woman in bed with him.

Her anger had propelled her out of his house that day, and home to her parents' ranch. Depression had set in and she'd slept and cried for a solid day. She hadn't had the energy to work with the horses that first week. She'd let the ranch hands do everything she was supposed to do, which made her even more depressed. Her friends stopped by in groups or singles. They told and retold the story of that night and assured her she was doing the right thing by making her fiancé sweat.

After Penny told them Jett's side of the story, though, their opinions wavered. *Try to work it out with him. It was just a mistake. He had to have been drunk. Maybe it happened the way he'd said it did. Valerie's never gotten over him. He's never done anything like this before. He's a good man. Give him another chance.*

She would have, too, if he'd bothered to contact

her. He hadn't called, hadn't tried to bust past her father's promise to keep him away from her. Nothing. Was it guilt? Had she been right—did Jett get wedding jitters? Had he found an easy way to shake loose of her?

After a week and a half of nothing from him, and far too much from her parents and friends, she needed a change. Calling her brother, she begged him to let her stay with him in Casper until she could find a wrangling job there.

Today, she'd packed up, despite her mother's tearful pleas, and her father's insistence that he would "*Beat some sense into that asshole.*"

She'd gotten fifty miles outside of town before she decided to turn around. She wouldn't slink away like an unwanted hound. She had to tell Jett she was leaving and see him one more time. His rough-cut face, those sky blue eyes, that tall, strong body that used to hold her so tightly.

Another crying binge threatened but the slam of the screen door jolted her out of it.

He took the stairs in one leap and walked toward her, holding something black. A book? Handing it to her, he dropped his head.

She tilted the leather-bound book toward the moon's glow. "Holy Bible."

He met her stare. "It was my mom's."

A lump caught in her throat. A year ago, his mother had died of a brain aneurism. Penny had heard about the ambulance racing to the ranch from a friend who worked at the hospital. She'd driven straight into town in her work clothes, smelling of horses and hay. She'd found Jett in the ER room, holding his mother's lifeless hand.

Penny had started crying and he'd held her. They'd taken a few moments to say goodbye to a wonderful woman, and Jett had insisted on driving them home to his ranch.

They'd sat on the couch, holding each other, watching the sunset. As it grew dark in the house, Jett had done something she'd never seen him do in the two years they'd been dating. He cried. She'd hugged him tight and let him pour out his grief, weeping her own silent tears. In those moments, she'd found a soul-deep love, an overpowering bond.

Looking up at him now, her lungs burned from trying to hold back the sob that fought to engulf her.

His jaw worked. Reaching out, he laid his hand on top of the book. "Penelope." He sucked in an uneven breath. "I swear on the bible…" His voice choked. "I swear on my mother's grave that I did not so much as touch Valerie, other than to push her away from me. That night, or any other night since I met you." He swallowed, his Adam's apple bobbing in his strong neck. "There has been no one but you."

Jett's mother had meant so much to him. This was a vow he would not make lightly. This was momentous. Staring at his chest, a sense of urgency overcame her. Had she been influenced by what her friends said they saw to the point where she lost her objectivity?

Like lightning flashes through her mind, she reviewed everything from Jett's perspective. He couldn't know Valerie had followed him outside. He'd walked back into the bar with her, but then turned around and walked righ out again. Oh, Lord, it was just as he said; completely circumstantial. With a jolt, she realized she'd believed him all along. She'd allowed her own insecurities to surface and drag her down into the drama. In her soul, she had always trusted him without reservation.

She stared into his eyes, losing her heart all over again to their perfect blue intensity. The ache that had gripped her chest for two long weeks disappeared, replaced by a swelling glow that consumed her. How could she ever have doubted him?

A tear slipped down her cheek as she slid her hand over his on the bible. "Jett." She tried to force a smile. "Forgive me for doubting you."

His mouth opened and he drew in a quick breath. Glancing up toward the stars, he paused a moment, then swept her into his arms.

"Oh, God, Penny." His hand burrowed across her scalp, holding her tight. His arm around her back nearly squeezed the oxygen from her.

But she didn't care. All that mattered was knowing he'd been faithful.

Tugging her head back, he looked into her eyes. "I love you."

She blinked back happy tears. "I love you, Jett." It was all she knew right now. The craziness of the last two weeks didn't matter.

His kiss possessed her, his tongue dominated her, touching inside her mouth, brushing the places that had gone without him for what seemed like an eternity. Her belly warmed as her body's craving for him woke from hibernation.

She took as much as she gave, twisting her tongue with his, tasting him, loving his mouth, his teeth, his lips. She barely breathed as she took him with insane abandon. Her man.

He slowed the kiss, pressing light brushes of his lips on her jaw and down her neck. "Come sit on the porch with me."

Her stomach jittered and her nipples pebbled. They'd spent many nights making love on the swing. "Oh, yes, Jett."

He picked her up in his strong arms, carrying her as if she was weightless.

Wrapping her arms around his neck, she pressed kisses along his hard jawline. Her fingers played with the ends of his hair. He hadn't been to the barber for his three-week trim and she liked it longer.

He sat on the porch swing and kept her on his lap. So many hours they'd sat like this talking about their future. When would things get back to the way they had been?

Running his hand up her thigh, he gazed at her with eyes so full of longing, she knew what would heal them.

"Make love to me, Jett."

His eyes closed for a moment and under her butt, his cock rose, thick and long. "Do we need to talk?" he ground out.

She smiled, loving how in touch with her sensitive side he'd become. "Love me first. There'll be years for us to talk."

"Baby." His hand slid under her shirt, cupping her breast through her bra. When he found her hard nipple, his thumb flicked back and forth over it. Tingling raced to her core, stinging need tightened deep inside her.

When she tugged at his shirt, he lifted his arms and let her strip it from him. The dark hair lightly furring his chest never failed to draw her fingers into it. So strong, his chest muscles flexed as he moved. He was a hard working man who did as much or more than any of his hired men.

His fingers unlatched her bra at her back and her shirt and bra joined his on the porch floor.

Warm, humid air brushed her sensitive skin. Latching his lips around her nipple, he suckled deeply.

"I'm starving for you," he growled as he moved to make love her other breast.

"Can't live..." The thought of what she'd almost thrown away choked her. "I couldn't live without you."

He lifted his head and she kissed him, showing all her passion for him, her desire for his loving. Nibbling on his lips, she knew she'd been through hell. From now on, her life with Jett would be heaven. She'd make it that way.

"Penny." His eyes darkened to a wild, midnight blue as his hand popped the button of her jeans and slid the zipper down. "I want to make love to you. I want to slide my cock inside you and show you how much I've missed you."

His words and intense stare sent jingles of lust to her pussy. Her lips swelled and creamed, making ready for his flesh. The sound of her own labored breathing proved how far gone she was. Shimmying onto his thighs, she unbuckled his belt, unbuttoned his jeans, and unzipped them.

"Lift up," she demanded, and slid his jeans down, freeing his big cock and hot balls. She pet him, tracing the veins she knew so well. Tickling the mushroom-shaped head she loved to lick, she spread the pre-cum across the tip. When she bent to taste him, he caught her face in his hands.

"Baby, it's been two weeks. If you touch that perfect mouth of yours on my cock, I'm going to explode."

Smiling, she bracketed his hands with hers.

"Later?"

"Fuck, yes. All night, Penny." His words held the promise of long, hot hours of sticky sex. Exactly what she needed. Just what she loved. His kiss sent prickles of desire to her clit, making her hips circle on his thighs when she wanted to be circling his hard, ready shaft.

Still locked in his kiss, Penny shimmied out of her jeans, kicking them and her shoes onto the pile of clothes.

He ended the kiss and he turned her to face out from the porch, the way they always did, so both of them could gaze over the land they loved.

Spreading her legs on the outsides of his, she let his hands on her hips guide her backward until his shaft nestled in her ass crack. She wriggled her hips, inviting him to take her there.

He groaned and his body shook for long seconds. "I need your pussy."

Her core convulsed in need as a fresh rush of juices slid from her opening.

Jett breathed deep. "I can smell you, baby." His hand slid over her belly and between her legs. His big, calloused fingers slipped through her curly hair to burrow into her wet folds. Easing one finger into her slit, his hips jerked. "I need you."

"Love me now. Please." Lifting herself, she pushed back, her ass hitting the solid wall of his abs. She reached between her legs and touched his hand.

He worked his finger in and out of her slit.

Delightful shimmies raced across her skin, swelling her lips, pulsing in her clit, and tugging at her breasts. She reached further back and grasped his cock, her hand barely able to circle its thickness.

"Slide your sweet cunt onto me, baby." His voice rumbled low and desperate as he pulled his finger from her opening. Using two fingers, he opened her folds, opened her to the evening air.

She touched the head of his cock to her slit. His hot skin burned her, made her crazy with the need to have him deep inside. Holding tight to his staff, she languidly eased down onto him.

Twisting, she gazed at him, their eyes locking, the moment both tender and sensual.

His width stretched her, the marvelous ache subsiding to pure pleasure. Inch by inch, she took him inside, willing her body to shift and make room for him.

His fingers stayed on her pussy, feeling himself enter her.

She laid her hand over his, her fingers on his, loving the slide of his cock moving into her.

"Feel that, Penny?" he growled, his eyes flashing wild desire. "That's everything I'll ever need. Just you and me, baby. Forever."

His words sent warm swirls to her heart. She loved this man and needed him with a soul-deep love. She trusted him implicitly, even when common sense told her not to.

When he was buried deep inside her, her hand brushed against his pubic bone, his springy, auburn hair tickled her hand. The feeling of complete fullness overtook her and she shivered with a pre-orgasmic blast that told her that this would be an unbelievable release.

He shivered as well, his eyes rolling back for a second then locking with hers again. All his love, his need, showing in his gaze.

Sighed, knowing they'd both break all records tonight.

She moved, circling her hips forward and back in the pattern she knew made him insane.

"Aw, yeah." His fingers tightened on their joined flesh. She did the same. The slick slide of their skin was mind altering.

Her juices flowed, drenching both their hands. She smelled her musk and her spine prickled with barbs of pleasure. "I'm not going to last…" she moaned as she responded by snapping off brain cells one by one. Closing her eyes, she dropped her head back onto his shoulder, arching her back, taking him as deep as she could get him.

"I'm hangin' by a thread here, too." His voice sounded manic. His hips jerked as if to punctuate his words. He slid his hand up until his fingers burrowed into her flesh, expertly finding her clit.

The light touch shot stinging waves of delight

flowing over her pussy lips, through her cunt, up her spine, then it exploded. Every cell in her brain sparked off as prickles of lust blinked inside her mind.

He cried out wrapped his arm across her body, lifting her so he could pump his throbbing cock into her, grunting with each plunge.

Her mind took her speeding through nothingness. Her body flushed and tingled as his hot shaft created friction along her spasming slit.

When he bit her neck and sucked, marking her as his own, she called his name into the night.

He pistoned his hips in a frantic rhythm, a race to find release. He stiffened. Inside her, his hot cum pulsed against her womb. He held her tight, thrumming her clit, sending her off on another shimmering ride that left her body scorched and sensitive.

"Aw, Penny," he whispered, kissing the shell of her ear. "I missed you."

Her body felt boneless, devoid of muscle. With much difficulty, she lifted her arms and laced her fingers through his hair. Her body quivered with aftershocks which sent his cock jerking inside her.

"This was what I needed," she murmured. "To wipe away the last weeks."

He sighed. "Back to reality, huh?" Easing his cock out of her, he stood her on the porch, got to his feet and hiked up his jeans, then reached back into the chest behind the swing. Pulling out the blanket they kept for cool nights, he wrapped her in it and settled back on the swing with her on his lap.

She snuggled her head into the crook of his neck. The view from the porch always gave her a sweet longing. One day, she'd be part of this ranch. Jett's wife, partner, lover, mother to his children. She'd almost lost it all and her throat clogged as she thanked heaven for making her turn around tonight and head back to her man.

"I was wrong to doubt you, Jett. Can you forgive me?"

His grip on her tightened. "I can, love. But I'd like to know…" He huffed out a sigh and shook his head.

"Anything. I'll tell you anything you want to know. Best to get it all out in the open right now."

His chest rose and fell a few times with his breathing. "Why couldn't you trust me before? Why did it take my swearing on a bible before you believed me?"

She heard the pain in his voice and wished she could go back to that morning, do everything differently. "At first, I was so angry, I could have slugged you."

"You should have. It might have diffused the situation."

Biting back a smile, she said, "No. I'd have probably broken my hand. Then I'd be twice as mad."

He chuckled and kissed the top of her head.

"After a few days, when I didn't hear from you, my mind slipped into worst case scenario. I imagined you wanted out of our engagement. I remembered times you'd seemed distant, and I blew them up in my mind until I thought you'd gotten cold feet."

"Huh." He resettled her to look into her eyes. "Like when?"

She shrugged. "When you had to go to Billings. You seemed upset with me."

"No, not with you. With my cattle broker."

Touching his face, she said, "I know that. But in my head…" She slid her hand down to his chest, feeling his strong heartbeat. "I'd somehow convinced myself you didn't want me any longer."

His brows furrowed. "I want you so damn bad, Penny, it makes me ache when you're not around." He took a deep breath. "But my damn pride."

She brushed a lock of hair from his forehead. "And you call me a stubborn redhead."

His brows furrowed. "I was an arrogant jerk. You said you wanted time, and I let you have it. I was angry, too. It killed me that you didn't believe me."

"Forgive me?" She forced back a wash of tears.

"Oh, baby. I forgive you. Will you forgive me? Stick around and help break me of that damn pride?"

Her heart swelled at his words. "You weren't too proud to bring out the bible."

He nodded. "I couldn't let you go."

"I'm glad you didn't. I know how much your

mother meant to you." She sucked in a choppy breath. "When you made that vow, everything became clear to me." She sat up. "I think you were set up. I think Valerie did this to get back at you for dumping her."

His eyebrow lifted. "I've been thinking the same thing. Especially the way she sat in my truck for two hours waiting for me. I'm going to talk to her—"

"No." She pressed her finger to his lips. "Now that we know what she's capable of, we'll just steer clear. And trust each other unquestioningly."

His gaze bore into hers. As if he were concocting something brilliant in his mind.

Penny cupped his cheek in her palm. "What's going on in your head?"

"I don't want to be without you ever again. I want you here with me."

She sighed. "I know how you feel, but I promised my parents." They were old-fashioned folks who knew that living in a small community meant gossip and scandal if one wasn't careful. She'd given them her word not to live with Jett until they were married.

His smile grew to light his face and his eyes twinkled. "Road trip." He stood, setting her on her feet.

"What? Right now?" She stepped closer to him, opening the blanket and pressing her breasts to his chest. "I thought we'd spend the night making up for lost time."

"Mmm. Tempting. But I have a better idea." He

picked up their clothes and held open the screen door for her. Grabbing the bible he'd carefully set aside, he followed her into the house. "Into the bedroom."

She walked barefoot along the polished hardwood floors and stepped into his room. "Tell me what's happening."

"We're going to shower. Then we're going to Vegas."

Her mouth dropped open. "Vegas? You feel like gambling?"

He shook his head, his eyes held a naughty gleam. "We're gettin' hitched."

Words failed her.

Reaching into the top dresser drawer, he pulled out a velvet box. He held it out to her.

She opened the box to find a wedding ring that matched her exquisite engagement ring. "Oh, Jett. It's beautiful. I didn't expect anything so elaborate." Set in white gold, diamonds sparkled around the entire band. She looked at him. "I don't know what to say."

He reached into the front pocket of his jeans and pulled out her engagement ring. Taking a knee in front of her, he held her left hand. "Will you marry me, Penelope Linder? Tomorrow?"

A giddy laugh bubbled out of her and she felt tears running from her eyes. "Jett McCord, I will marry you. Tomorrow."

He slipped the ring on her finger and stood to plant a kiss on her lips.

"Why the urgency?"

He nodded toward the driveway. "You're all packed. We'll just shower, hop in your car, and go. We can stop at a hotel in a few hours. Get some rest, some sex..." He rubbed the bulge in his jeans against her blanket-clad mound. "Some food, and make it to Vegas by sunset tomorrow."

Her cheeks hurt from smiling so wide. "I should call my parents and let them—"

"When we're on the road. When it's too late for you to change your mind."

"I won't change my mind, but they'll be disappointed."

"Let them throw you that big-ass wedding and reception next spring. I don't mind marrying you twice."

She shrugged and shook her head. "I don't know what's gotten into you, Jett." She dropped her blanket and wrapped her arms around his neck. "But I love it." She kissed him and smiled. "I can't wait to be your wife."

"When we get back, we'll just move you right in here." His hands smoothed down her back to her butt. Grabbing a hold, he said, "Then we can get started on the first of our red-headed babies."

Smoothing his hair off his forehead, she said, "Stubborn red-headed babies, knowing our DNA."

~ ~ ~ ~

Takin' a Chance

Garth Murphy leaned his arms on the top rail of the metal fence surrounding the arena floor. The barrel racers were up next. The Friday night rodeo crowd shouted encouragement as the first woman guided her horse around the three red plastic drums.

The other bullfighters had gone backstage to rest before the short go began. He'd head back, too, after he watched *her* ride.

Pulling his hat off, he looked up at the scoreboard. His blond, curly hair sprang free and he ran a hand through to tame it out of his eyes. Where were they, again? Arizona? Yeah, Buckeye, Arizona. The days had started flowing into each other about a week ago. It'd been a long tour. Only made bearable at the venues where Heather competed.

"And our next racer is Heather Ehrlich, from Hurricane, Utah, riding Whipcord."

Garth stood tall, gripping the metal railing.

Heather and her buckskin quarter horse, blasted out of the gate. Her black braids flew behind her from under her red cowgirl hat. Whipcord knew what to do, and with Heather's strong, sure hand, they took the first barrel without an error. Whipcord kicked up dirt as she rounded the second barrel.

Garth's heart beat faster at the determined look on Heather's face. Her dark, full lips pressed tight in concentration. If sheer will could win a contest, she'd take first place every time. Which she did, for the most part. His gaze dropped to her breasts covered in the white and red checkered shirt she always wore for luck. Those perfect C-cups bounced just enough to start a fire behind the fly of his loose bullfighter shorts, turning his athletic supporter painful.

His mouth watered so viciously for a taste of her, he had to swallow twice.

When Whipcord slid toward the third barrel, Garth thought it was over. The crowd gasped. Knocking over a drum would add penalty time to her score. Heather shifted her body weight to pull the horse through, leaving the barrel upright. Damn, she was good.

Cheers rang out as she crossed the electric eye and slowed to a trot back behind the chutes.

Garth hadn't realized he was holding his breath. He drew in a mighty gulp of air as the announcer let them know Heather was currently in first place.

Settling his hat on his head, he walked back where she corralled her horse.

Heather slid down off the saddle and gave Whipcord a hug, talking to him in her sweet voice.

What he wouldn't give to hear her talk to *him* like that. To wrap her arms around *his* neck. Garth shook his head. He'd known Heather for a year, and even though some sort of electric charge sparked between them, it couldn't happen.

She was twenty-eight. Ten years younger than him. A lot of men dated younger women, but he'd been brought up by a mother who, from an early age, drilled into him how wrong that was—after her husband left her for a younger gal.

When he walked up to the corral fence, she spotted him. Her smile broke across her whole face. Her dark eyes shone in the arena lighting. Her skin was a light mocha color, a blessing from her Ute mother and her German father.

Her kindness was her best feature, though. She spent long hours helping young barrel racers perfect their rides. She cheered on her competition and pep talked the losers out of their gloom. She had a smile for everyone, and didn't hesitate to tease the rough stock cowboys with the superiority of barrel racing.

"Hi, Garth. You doing okay?"

His hand went to where his safety vest covered his ribs. A bull had tried to shish kebab him earlier. "A little tender. Nothing major."

She made a disbelieving face. "Jeez-oh-Petes. You were gored." Taking the saddle and blanket off her horse, she picked up a brush. "You have it looked at, anyway?"

"No need." He grinned. "I've had worse."

She shrugged as she stroked the brush along Whipcord's flank. "Tough guy."

He liked how she worried about him. Maybe that's what attracted him to her. He had nobody else who cared. A couple brothers he saw once or twice a year. An ex-wife somewhere. Hadn't had a date in a hell of a long time. Even though Heather spread her positive energy among all the contestants, she seemed to reserve an extra large portion for him.

Heather turned. "You goin' to the dance tonight after the rodeo?"

There was a country band playing out under the stars. He'd love to take her. Pull her into his arms for a slow two-step. "Na." He had to remember the age difference. The life experience difference. He'd been working the rodeo since he dropped out of high school at seventeen. Traveling, seeing the country, working his way up from stall mucker to bullfighter. Which he was getting too damn old for.

Heather's life was the opposite of his. She came from a rich family. Whipcord was one of the top horses in the sport. A contingent of her relatives usually showed up at every event.

He braced a booted foot on the bottom rail and leaned his forearms on the top. "That's for you young kids."

She froze, sucked in a huge breath, and let it out with a dramatic sigh. Piercing him with a stare that could kill, she pointed the brush at him. "Why do you always do that?"

His eyes shifted left then right before locking with hers. "Do what?"

"Make yourself out to be an old man." She shook

her head and went back to grooming Whipcord.

"Compared to you, I am an old man." It hurt to admit it.

Heather's arms dropped to her sides. Turning slowly, she narrowed her eyes. "Is that what's been holding you back?"

His heart thumped a couple times. What was she asking? "Holding me back?"

Taking a step toward him, she pushed her hat off her head. The stampede strap caught it at her neck. "From me."

Garth slid his foot off the rail, dropped his arms, and stood straight. She was different tonight. More aggressive, and he liked it. His breath came faster. "From you?" Did he sound like a goddamn parrot?

She jammed her fists into her hips. "All this time, I told myself you weren't interested."

Locking his jaw, he held back what he wanted to say. *I'm so fucking interested, I dream of you. Get off thinking of you. Can't stand to look at another woman because of you.*

Slow as molasses, her mouth curved up into a smile. Her eyes took on a wicked gleam. Her fists went to flat palms against her jeans and slid down her round hips to her toned thighs. "You feel the same way about me as I feel about you." Biting her lower lip, she walked toward him, stopping on the other side of metal rail fence from him. "Admit it."

Garth stared into eyes so dark, they drew him out

into a moonlit night. Just the two of them, no social constraints, no improprieties to worry about, no rodeo code of behavior standing between them. "I'm ten years older than you."

That had her brows lifting. "No." She smiled and shook her head. "You aren't thirty eight." Her brows drew together. "Are you really?"

Placing his hands on the top pipe of the fence, he steadied himself. His heart didn't know what to do. Race with excitement, or slow to a dull thud with dejection. "I am."

She stepped forward, crossing her arms over the top rail between his hands. "You don't look older than thirty." Her gaze dropped down his body. "I've seen you in street clothes. You have the build of an athlete." She reached out and touched his chest. The protective vest under his shirt prevented him from feeling the warmth of her palm. "You're young at heart," she whispered.

Of their own accord, his feet moved closer to the fence until he looked down into her eyes. He could fall for this woman. Hell, he was already more than halfway there. "Yeah, but in fifty years, I'll be…"

"Fifty years?" She tipped her head and smiled a teasing grin. "You've already planned our life out fifty years?"

He shook his head. "You—"

"Congratulations, Heather." A female voice interrupted from behind him. "Good ride today."

She blinked a couple times and looked past him. "Thanks. Who won?"

The other woman laughed. "You did, hun. But I guess you didn't hear, with all the turtle-dovin' goin' on back here."

Heather smiled and red crept onto her cheeks. When she glanced at him, Garth nearly sighed. Beautiful. Smart. Talented. He wanted her for more than just sex. He liked being around her.

"Congratulations." He patted her arm. It felt awkward, and her half-grin told him she felt the same.

"I don't even get a hug?" Stepping on the bottom rail, she boosted herself to eye-level with him and grasped his shoulders.

He automatically wrapped his arms around her to keep her from slipping. His hands settled on muscle under warm, soft flesh. God, she was sexy. When he opened his mouth to ask what the hell she was doing, she moved closer.

Their cheeks brushed as she tugged him tighter.

A wave of heat flooded his groin, stiffening his cock and energizing his balls. Thankfully, the fence stood between their bodies. Breathing deep, he smelled her scent. Soap, leather, horse and sweet spices. The urge to tip his head and taste the flesh of her neck nearly sidelined him.

"Come to the dance," she whispered warm and gentle in his ear.

His gut tensed, hearing the desire in her voice. He

had to force his arms from around her. Helping her down on the other side of the fence, he slid his hands from her arms. "No promises."

Her head dropped then she glanced up at him. "I'm not asking for promises. Just one night." She turned and bent to pick up her brush. "I'll be waiting for you."

Ah, shit. His hands fisted, wanting those round, tight ass cheeks of her in his palms. Needing her body pressed naked to his. He wished for one night, and a whole hell of a lot more.

"Garth, let's go!" Another bullfighter walked past him on the way into the arena.

He wanted to say more to her, but it would have to wait.

After the bull riding finished, Garth changed into boots and jeans, a gray shirt and a black Stetson. Deliberately walking past where the band was tuning up, he drove to the bar where the other bullfighters planned to meet. Sitting around a big table talking aches, pains, broken bones, and rank bulls usually helped make the night go faster. But not tonight.

His mind was on the dance going on back at the equine center. She was waiting for him. After downing one beer, he stood. "I'm heading out." The thought of Heather standing around watching for him made his gut ache.

His buddies stared at him. He was usually one of the last to leave. With nowhere to go and no one to get back to, he regularly stayed until last call, spending the last few hours sobering up so he could drive his friends back to the hotel.

"Got a date?"

He shrugged. "Sort of."

"Which way are you going?" one of the guys, Craig, asked.

"Back to the equestrian center. I…forgot something." Like his ethics. "Need a lift?"

"Yeah." Craig stood and polished off his brew. "I thought I'd check out the dance."

A man laughed. "That's for the young bucks."

"Yeah, Craig," someone else said. "You'll be the oldest guy there."

Shit. *He'd* be the oldest guy there. Maybe this wasn't such a good idea.

Craig flipped them off. Turning toward the door, he said, "Let's go."

In the truck, Garth changed his mind back and forth about two dozen times. He'd think of Heather looking around, hoping he'd show up and want to get there fast. Then he'd think about all the cowboys her own age and wondered if it would be better to leave her there alone, so she could find someone else.

They parked and walked toward the outdoor stage. The dance floor was huge, with strings of lights hanging over it, strung between the tree branches. He glanced around the crowd but didn't see Heather.

"Let me buy you a beer." Craig steered them

toward the portable bar.

"Yeah. Sure." They made their way through the groups of cowboys, cowgirls, and buckle bunnies.

"Hey, it's the bullfighters!" One of the bareback riders clapped them both on the back. "Lemme buy you old timers a drink."

****

"Asswaffle," she murmured. Heather couldn't believe the stupid bronc rider had called Garth "old." The three men stood next to the bar with cans of beer in their hands. Garth Murphy was the bravest man she'd ever met in rodeo. He was the best bullfighter out there, jumping in to save riders as well as other bullfighters more often than any others did.

A quiet, reserved man with a strength that drew her in. She'd heard about all the times he'd played sober cab to rodeo folk. They could call him any time of the night and he'd drive off to help them. Between rides, he'd talk to the kids in the stands, give them little toys that he kept in his pockets. How could anyone be so disrespectful to such a wonderful human being?

She straightened her spine and walked toward them. "Here goes."

Garth's gaze shot to hers, traveled down her body then back up. She'd freed her hair from the braids and it hung thick and wavy down her back to nearly her ass. Her purple T-shirt matched her cowgirl boots, and her jeans had sexy beading on the back pockets.

If this didn't get his attention, nothing would.

Standing in front of them, she took a breath. "Evenin', gentlemen."

They each tipped their hats. "Evenin'."

The bronc rider stepped closer, wobbling a little. The smell of alcohol preceded him. "Can I buy you a beer, Miss Heather?"

"No thank you." What was his name, again?

The kid got closer. "Then maybe you want to dance with me." His grin told her he'd like to do that and a whole lot more.

She opened her mouth to refuse and tell him to back off.

Garth interjected his arm between her and the bronc rider, and wrapped it across her back. "I believe I owe Miss Heather a drink." He shot the kid a warning glare.

Craig let out a laugh.

The kid stepped back and scratched his head under his cowboy hat.

Garth's hand slid down to her lower back. The gesture was gentlemanly and innocuous. But to her, the feel of him touching her so firmly, guiding her so masterfully to the farthest end of the bar sent chills racing in her spine.

They stopped and he removed his hand, gesturing to the bartender. Looking into her eyes, he asked, "Beer? Wine?"

The blue of his gaze melted her insides. "What

you're having is fine."

He ordered two more. Glancing around the dance floor, his mouth turned down. "Young crowd tonight."

"Mm hm." She wasn't going to revisit the age thing again. "By this time of the night, the older couples have danced themselves out and gone home."

He paid for their beer and handed one to her.

She grinned up at him. "Thank you." Her belly tightened with a warm dose of lust as he smiled at her. "And thank you for saving me from the buckaroo."

He nodded. "He's not a bad guy. Just a little over the limit tonight."

"I don't know him very well. He's new this year."

He stiffened and his smile faded. "I didn't get into the middle of something, did I?"

It took a second for her to figure out what he was saying. She pointed to her chest. "Me?" She pointed to the kid who stood talking with Craig. "And buckaroo?"

"He's probably closer to your…generation." He stared off at the boy.

Damn him. What did she have to do to convince him his age wasn't an issue? "Bite me," she mumbled and downed half her beer.

"Whoa. Thirsty?"

Setting down the half-empty can, she crossed her arms and aimed a serious look at him. "The kid is nineteen. There's nearly the same age difference between him and me, and between me and you." She could feel her German temper boiling up. "And you're trying to hook me up with him?"

His brows rose a little higher with each word she ground out. "I didn't—"

She leaned closer and kept her voice a hiss. "Do you have any idea how insulting that is?" Especially since she'd practically thrown herself at Garth after her ride tonight. But she'd had to. She had so little time left to get him to realize how she felt about him. And how *he* felt about *her*.

"Now, hold on." He set down his beer. "I'm just pointing out that some of these young guys have a lot to offer."

Heather flung up her hands with a heavy puff of breath and stalked off toward the equine center. People moved out of her way as she stomped dirt with her boots and grumbled to herself about a damn stubborn cowboy who couldn't make up his mind. She found the paved path that led to the building and walked with purpose toward it.

"Heather." Garth's booted feet clomped loudly as he came up behind her. "I didn't mean to rile you."

She'd just wanted to get away. "I don't want to argue."

"Stop a minute. Let's talk."

She needed time to think, and as long as he was close… "I'm going to check on Whipcord."

They walked the next few yards in silence.

When she reached for the door handle, Garth's arm came around her and tugged it open, letting her enter first.

The scent of hay and manure mixed with the smell of horse always calmed her nerves and set her right again. "I'm sorry, Garth." She went right to Whipcord's corral. It could use a cleaning, and her baby would appreciate some oats and fresh water. She pet Whipcord's nose, easing her frustration even further. "I didn't mean to cause a scene."

A bitter laugh came from him.

She turned to find him standing stiffly, his booted feed spread, his hands at his side in fists. "I don't give a shit about what people think, Heather."

Her heart thumped a wild beat. He'd never seemed as masculine, as sexy, as he did right now. She liked this side of him. She stepped closer. "Then why do you worry about our age difference?"

His jaw worked for a minute. "It just ain't right. You're young, just getting into barrel racing. I'm contemplating retiring. Buying a ranch somewhere and staying put."

Now it was her turn to laugh. "I'm young?" She shook her head. "In this business, twenty-eight is getting a little old." She poked her finger into his chest. "And you have no idea what my goals are, Garth. I've almost completed my masters in business. I want to open a barrel racing school. On a stud farm where I can breed quarter horses and train them myself." She puffed out a breath. "I'm only finishing this season to try and get another championship to prove my credentials for teaching."

His brow furrowed. "I didn't know you were in school."

"I don't talk about it around here. It makes people uncomfortable."

He glanced down. "Yeah. I can see that."

Now she'd gone over the top with him. A while back, she'd let it slip that her parents were wealthy. And her advanced degree had to intimidate someone who had never gotten the chance to go to college. "You're not hearing what I'm saying."

He looked at her, questions in his eyes.

"I'm trying to explain to you how mature I am for a twenty-eight year old, and all you hear is that I'm gonna have an MBA."

"And I won't."

She groaned.

"Doesn't that bother you, Heather?" He grabbed her arms, his big hands wrapping around her biceps. "Not only am I older, not only do I not have a college degree of any sort, but…" His lips thinned as his eyes dropped. "I never graduated high school."

"That doesn't matter to—"

He shook her once, gently, his eyes searching hers. "It should matter to you."

"Ma'am?" a man said from behind him. "Is

everything okay here?"

Garth dropped his hands and they turned toward the security guard.

"I'm okay, thank you." She shrugged. "Just a lover's quarrel."

Garth looked at her, his expression un-amused.

"Take it outside, okay folks?"

Garth nodded. "Sorry." Placing his hand on her lower back, he walked her to the door, pushed it open for her, and followed her out.

The night air was warm and dry, a desert evening. A cicada buzzed in a mesquite tree. The band played a slow song, and her chest ached with the need to dance with him. To be held in his arms. She knew he wouldn't ask her to join him on the dance floor but maybe…

She veered toward the grove of trees just off to the side of the arena.

"Where are you going?"

Walking backward, she smiled. "Come and see."

He pulled his black cowboy hat off his head and ran his fingers through that gorgeous bush of curly blond hair. Resettling the hat on his head, he let out a huff and stomped after her.

When he reached the dark privacy of the trees, she made her move. She flattened herself against him, her hands on his hard biceps.

He grunted and stiffened.

"Dance with me, cowboy." Her arms snaked

around his neck.

He gripped her elbows as if he would pull her off him. After a second, his hands slid down to her shoulders then over her back. Finally, his arms wrapped around her.

Her soul cried, *"Heaven"* as he pulled her tighter.

He moved his body, swaying them from side to side. "You know what?"

"What?" She followed his rhythm, her tummy brushing against his big belt buckle. Every inch of her that touched him tingled and warmed.

"You're starting to annoy me." His voice said otherwise as he bent his head and pressed his face into her hair, inhaling deeply.

"Good." Against her belly a rise pressed, hard and hot. Her core fluttered and warmed, knowing the hard-on was for her, only.

He tucked her hair behind her left ear. "Why is that good?" His warm words ticked her ear, sending a buzz to her breasts, pebbling her nipples.

"At least you're not ignoring me any longer." Tipping her head, she offered him her neck.

With a moan, he kissed her earlobe, then her neck.

Chills lanced down her spine.

"How could I ignore you…" His lips nibbled along her jawline. "When you're so perfect?"

Perfect? Her? "Huh?"

He tunneled his fingers into her hair, along her scalp, tipping her head up. "Perfect." His eyes blazed blue flame and he stopped dancing, pressing his erection into her stomach.

Opening her mouth, she flicked her tongue over her bottom lip. "I'm not perfect."

"Goddamnit. Yes you are." He released her, falling back a step. "I keep forgetting why I can't take advantage of you."

Her arms dropped from his shoulders, leaving her cold and alone. "You mean, take advantage of my youth and naiveté?"

He pulled off his hat and slapped it against his leg. "More than that. You're from an important family, you're smart, and you've won how many championships?" He shook his head. "I like you, Heather. A hell of a lot. But I don't think I'm the man for you."

Her head dropped forward, hiding the flood of moisture in her eyes. She'd tried everything to get his attention. She'd been patient for a year, waiting for him to make a move. She'd teased him, flattered him, hinted blatantly. Now, today, when time was running short, she'd tried arguing with him, hoping to get his dander up. It didn't work.

Her last ploy, seduction under the mesquite tree, had gone wrong, too. She had to admire him, though. He could have used her. Slept with her on his terms then dropped her when things got too intense. But that wasn't Garth Murphy. He was a gentleman.

"Fine." She looked into his eyes. "I understand.

You don't think we'd fit into each other's world."

She turned away but swung her head around to give him one last chance.

His eyes were closed, his lips pulled into a tight line, and his hand fisted at his side. This did not look like a man who didn't want the woman in front of him.

This looked like a man who was trying to do the right thing. At least, what he thought was the right thing. "Garth?"

He opened his eyes.

She saw pain and desire on his face.

"I'm going to say goodnight to Whipcord."

He stepped forward. "I'll wait with you."

"No." She held out a hand, nearly touching him, but not quite. "I'll have the guard walk me to my truck."

"Heather, I…"

She shook her head. "Good night." She turned and walked away.

An hour later, she pulled into the parking lot of the Hitchin' Post Motel. As she cruised toward the office, she noticed Garth's truck parked in front of room seventeen. A light showed through the gap in the curtain. She parked and walked into the office. When she rang the bell, a young boy came out of the back room.

"I've got a reservation." She gave him the details then asked, "Is eighteen available?"

He typed on the computer. "Yep. Just rented seventeen to a cowboy, though. Would you rather be down closer to the office? I can give you a quieter room."

"No thanks." The idea of being right next to Garth made her mostly happy and a portion sad. "Eighteen would be perfect."

After pulling her rig in front of her room, she grabbed her suitcase and used the key card to enter. Bonus! The rooms had adjoining doors. She pressed her ear to her side. Muted voices carried, along with soft music. Was he watching television?

She backed up to the bed and sat. What the heck was she doing? He'd said no. A couple times. And he'd had good reasons behind his refusals, too.

No, not *good* reasons. Just excuses. Reasons why he thought he wasn't good enough for her. Why he was too old for her. Jiminy Christmas, where did that low self-esteem come from? Or was it overblown gentleman-ness?

She bit her thumbnail. She had to give this one more try, but how? What more could she do? What hadn't she said? "Well, hell, Miss Heather. You never told him why he *is* good enough for you." Was it just that simple? Her plan of action ready to roll, she jumped up from the bed and slowly, silently opened her connecting door. Pressing her ear against his door, she held her breath.

He flipped channels, stopping briefly on sports

news before settling on some cheesy movie. Sounded like a sex scene.

Great. He wouldn't sleep with her, but he'd watch that crap.

"Fucking son of a cock," he growled and something hit the bed, something like a fist. The bedsprings squeaked. Very near where she stood, the sound of someone digging in ice reached her, then the pop of a can opening. He paced, drinking and burping loudly.

She had to hold back a giggle. Her father was the same way. He never burped loud like that unless he thought he was alone.

The sound of a can being crushed in a strong fist was followed by the aluminum hitting the bottom of a trashcan. The bedsprings squeaked again. He groaned. "What the fuck did I do?" The sound of another fist hitting the mattress made her lift her hand to knock.

She stopped. Was he regretting telling her no?

She needed to do this just right or he wouldn't budge that stubborn mind of his. She eased the door closed but didn't lock it. Unzipping her suitcase, she grabbed a condom and slid it into her pocket. From her wallet, she pulled a fifty-dollar bill. She bit her lower lip, stuck the fifty back in, and pulled out a hundred. If her father knew what she was planning to do with the emergency money he made her carry, he'd sit her down and give her a two-hour lecture.

****

Garth sat on his bed in his red boxer briefs, pillows propping him against the headboard. He wished to hell he'd handled tonight different. He could have taken her out for a late dinner. They could have talked. But no, he'd tried to do it clean and painless.

"Shit." The pain he'd seen in her eyes just before she'd walked away nearly broke him in half.

Staring at the television, he made himself concentrate on the cable channel. The R-rated shot of the man in bed with the woman stirred something low in his groin. That could have been him tonight. With Heather.

Closing his eyes, he touched his cock. His mind saw her full lips, her tight ass, those perfectly shaped breasts. A jolt of action struck him low and he reached down to tug at his balls.

Three knocks sounded and his outside door swung open. He'd just sat up when he recognized Heather.

"Don't you move, Garth Murphy," she warned, throwing the keycard on the little table under the window and slamming the door behind her.

"What are you—"

"And don't say a word until I finish what I have to say." Her fists went to her hips. Her hair hung wild and silky. Her eyes blazed.

Fuck. Him. He'd never seen anything that sexy in his life. He couldn't help the smile that crossed his face. Whatever demon had gotten a hold of her was going to have its say.

He leaned back against the headboard, crossed his arms, crossed his ankles, and nodded. "Say your piece, woman."

She blinked a couple times. Had she expected him to refuse to hear her? Hell. He'd been trying to figure out how to fix this for the last hour, where to find her, and now…here she was.

"How did you get in here?" He pointed to the card on the table.

"Bribed the desk clerk."

"Uh huh." He lifted a brow. "Sounds like your style."

"I…" Her brow crinkled. "What?" She waved her hands around. "No, never mind. You're going to listen to me this time."

"All right. Shoot, cowgirl."

She sucked in a breath and let it out in a long, steady stream. "You don't know who you are."

He narrowed his eyes. "And you do?"

She smirked. "Yes, I do. And I'm going to tell you."

"This'll be interesting."

"First." She held up her index finger. "You're the bravest bullfighter I've ever seen. You risk it all to save the riders, the other fighters."

"It's my job—"

She slashed air. "Zzzzt."

He shut his mouth, a grin bubbling around inside him. She made him crazy, in a good way.

"Two. You care for everybody you work with. You go visit them in the hospital when they're injured. You drive them home if they've had too much to drink. You help out wherever you're needed."

He watched her, amazed at her tenacity. She wasn't going to give up on him.

Thank God!

"Three." She blinked. "You're so nice to the kids." Her voice was softer. "The rodeo folks' kids, the kids in the stands. You're a kind person. You'd make such a…"

Was she going to say, "*A good father?*" He could imagine them with kids. Ponies. Mini-vans. Puppies.

"Three."

"This would be number four."

She sighed. "Three and a half. You are a good man. You're quiet but strong. You're all man. Sexy and wonderful." Her voice slid into a soft purr.

His cock responded immediately. He slid one foot up the bed, hoping his bent leg would hide what was happening in his drawers.

"Four. I'm not perfect. Not by a country mile. I have days when I can't get my undies out of a bundle. I get frustrated sometimes. I put my goals above my personal relationships."

"I'm sorry I called you perfect." He shook his

head, straining to comprehend the irony in that apology.

She was silent for a while.

"Is there a number five?"

She nodded. "Five. Your moral values and integrity are what draws me to you." She stepped closer to the bed. "And what has kept you from me all this time."

"True. But a man can't change his values to accommodate his desires."

"Wow. That's so fucking deep."

He laughed. "I've never heard you swear before."

She shrugged. "I've never heard you say anything that fucking deep before." She bit her thumbnail for a second then dropped her hand. "I'm not looking for a one-night thing. But I'm not asking you to marry me, either."

Goddamn. Wouldn't that be amazing.

"Garth. All I'm asking you to do is give us a try. It can be on your terms. You call me when you want to see me. And if you don't call, I won't bother you."

"Sweetheart."

"No." She held up a hand. "Let me finish. I checked my rankings for the season. I've already clinched the championship."

"Congratulations."

"Thanks, but," she bit her lip. "What I'm getting at is, I don't have to compete any more this season. I'm going back to Utah to work on my master's thesis."

He didn't like the sound of that. There were two more rodeos. He'd miss her.

"That way, no one would have to know we're seeing each other. Your secret would be safe."

He ran his fingers through his hair. "I told you. I don't care what people think."

"I know you did, and I believe you. But it'll be easier to keep our relationship a secret until we know if it's going to work."

He couldn't keep up with her train of thought. "Just lay it on the line, Heather. What do you want from me?"

She dug in her pocket and pulled out a foil packet. A condom? She tossed it onto the bed. "Decide, Garth. Do you want me?" She gestured to the television where a man had his woman pressed against a wall, kissing her with enthusiasm. "Or do you want a bottle of lube and your hairy right hand?"

The laugh that escaped his throat surprised them both. In less than a second, he was out of bed. "I want you so goddamn much, Heather Ehrlich, I don't know where to start." Pulling her against him, he kissed her, his lips on hers connected directly to his shaft. Heat pumped into it, through his balls, racing up and down his spine.

He tasted her lips first, sweet and soft. Testing the insides of her lips, he ran his tongue along her teeth. When her tongue lapped against his, his hips jerked, sending his hard staff pumping into her belly.

She took sweet little tastes of his mouth, then boldly stroked his tongue and sucked it, circling the tip as if she was showing him what she'd do to his cock.

"You've got too many clothes on." He tugged at the hem of her shirt then skinned it off her. "Ah, nice." Her see-through purple bra taunted him. Leaning down, he sucked her tight little nipple through the cloth. Then the other one, loving the texture of the fabric.

She groaned and reached behind her, unhooking the bra and slipping out of it. "Do that again."

He obliged, taking one sweet nipple into his mouth and playing his fingers against the other.

Reaching down, she stroked his erection.

He nearly shot off. "It's been a while for me, sweetheart. Let's take this slow."

"Plus you were watching porn just now." She winked. "That has to get you juiced up."

He cupped her cheeks. "It wasn't porn, and I was thinking of you the whole time."

She laughed once then sobered at his intense stare. "You're serious. Wow."

"Uh huh." His hands raced to the button of her jeans. Unfastening, unzipping them, he tugged them down her legs, revealing her see-through purple bikini panties. "Sexy." He grinned. "Naughty."

"For you." Her eyes held more emotion than he could identify in his current state.

Kissing her wildly, letting his raging desire loose in the kiss, he slid his hands down her back and under her panties to cup her round, firm ass. "I've dreamed of this."

She sighed and slipped her hands under the waistband at his back, grasping his ass. "I want to bite this." Her eyes flashed wicked.

His brows lifted and a laugh escaped. "You're a wild one. I have a feeling you're going to show me a few new tricks." He waited for her to comment on the *Old dog, new trick* cliché, but she didn't. It was a sore spot between them, and one he'd have to learn to let go of.

"I think you know a few things that'll impress me, too." She bent and hauled his briefs down his thighs to his ankles.

His cock bounced wildly, enjoying the fresh air and freedom.

As she came back up, she stopped at his shaft and looked up at him. Her smile, the lick of her tongue on her lip, shot a roaring burn to his gut, his balls, and his penis.

When her tongue shot out to touch his head, his body flared like tiny campfires burned at each nerve ending.

Taking her shoulders, he stood her up straight. "My turn." He kissed the perfect divide between her plump breasts and peppered kisses down her stomach, around her belly button, and lower to the elastic band of her panties.

Sneaking his index fingers under the elastic, he rubbed back and forth across her soft, tan skin. From his viewpoint, he could see the hairs of her mound, closely trimmed and black as night. He bit his tongue between his teeth and glanced up at her.

Her mouth was open, her breath panting between her full lips. Her half-closed eyelids couldn't hide the unfocused, dilated darkness of her eyes.

Easing her panties down, he stared into her gaze. "I want to eat you. I want to taste and suck you, and bite and lick…"

She cried out and grabbed his shoulders, her body shuddering.

Quickly, he eased her panties off and stood. Reaching down, he hauled her up into his arms and stepped to the bed.

The feel of her, in his arms, in his power, under his control, struck him low with a blaze of lust, but rattled his chest with a gush of tenderness. She trusted him. She wanted him. She'd talked about a future for them. What a lucky bastard he was.

Laying her carefully on the bed, he started to kneel on the floor next to her, intent on spreading her thighs and feasting on her pussy. But he changed his mind. He wanted to start off this night with a bang. With something she'd remember forever.

Walking to the other side of the bed, he lay down opposite her, his face at her thighs.

"Garth. You are..." She sighed. "Yes." She reached for his cock, wrapping her hot fingers around his length.

His balls pumped a tiny squirt of pre-come which she lapped at hungrily. The combination of her hand squeezing him and her tongue teasing would send him to an early blast-off. He had to concentrate on...her sweet pussy.

He tugged her hip until she lay on her side and lifted her top leg, bending her knee to open her pussy to his gaze. "You're fabulous, sweetheart." Her dark hair covered a sleek mound, her lips opened to reveal a slick, glistening slit. Grasping her ass cheek with one hand, he breathed to slow himself down then pressed his lips against her opening.

She jerked then shivered, goose bumps rose on her thighs. "I like that, Garth."

"I know you do. You're wet and quivering. You know I'm going to make you come."

Letting out a squeal, her body shimmied for long seconds. "It won't take much."

He pumped his hips, letting her hand slide up and down his erection. "Probably even less to get me there."

Her mouth covered his head then slid down to take him all the way in, halfway down her throat.

His eyes rolled back as his balls tightened. His ass clenched, and he had to rip himself back from the orgasm that threatened to rage through him. Licking his lips, he tasted her juices and set his goal on making her come first.

Garth lapped at her folds, tasting her sweetness, his tongue dove deep into her slit, exploring the softness, the smooth spots, the puckered areas. She tasted like nothing he'd ever had, and everything he wanted to possess.

She sucked him, teasing with her tongue. Then, using her hand to pump him nearly into oblivion, she licked his balls with firm strokes and crazy circles. His lower back clenched and threatened to release his cum right that second.

Focusing, he got busy suckling her, circling her pussy lips with nips and kisses and licks. Sliding his hand between her legs from behind, he let his fingers take over while he eased his head forward, toward her little bud. He found her clit hiding under its hood, hard and hot. Stroking it with his tongue, he nearly lost her as her hips pumped wildly.

He took her clit between his lips, sucking and tonguing it wildly. His hand cupped over her slit, massaging the cream that flowed sweetly from her. Sliding a finger deep into her opening, he caught his breath at her tightness, the rhythmic pulsing inside her.

She cried out and he knew she was there. His mouth found a beat to match her thrusting hips. He eased a second finger into her core. She tensed and shuddered as her orgasm hit.

But she wouldn't leave him behind. Deep throating him, she rammed him into her mouth, over and over she took him fully until he could feel her chin brushing his pubic bone. Flashes of heat tore up his spine signaling his brain.

Against his hand, her core convulsed. Quick spasms tightened around his fingers.

His mind went nuclear, exploding with the heat and colors of a raging orgasm. Flames licked at his lower back, his cock.

When she tugged at his balls, powerful surges of cum raced from his staff straight down her throat. His body heated as the blaze surrounded him, setting his skin tingling and showing flares of red behind his eyelids. With each of her swallows, his head pulsed and his brain rattled until there was nothing left inside him, she'd take it all. Slowly his shaking body calmed, his mind lazily returned to reality, and his body temperature dropped from solar hot to afterglow steaming.

Easing his tongue into a slow pulse, then a soft blanket over her clit, he pulled his dripping fingers from her slit.

****

Heather had never experienced an orgasm that wild, especially while giving her man a full-throttle orgasm like the one Garth and just had. She licked at the drop of cum dangling from his head and looked down her body to see him lapping at her pussy, eating up all her juices.

When he backed away and looked at her, they both smiled.

"You do have some tricks," she purred. She'd had no idea he'd be this amazing in bed. Her past lovers had never come close. This man had mega-talent.

He rearranged himself so his head rested on the pillow next to hers and pulled her tightly against him, looking deep into her eyes. "That's a moment I'll never forget."

She smiled. "Me either. The highpoint of my love life."

He laughed, a slow rolling chuckle. "The highpoint so far. My goal will be to top it. On a regular basis."

Sliding her hand over his shoulder then up onto his head to play in his hair, she grinned. "Goals are so important."

Kissing her quickly, he wrapped her in his arms. "Tell me about your goals. You'd mentioned a ranch."

"Mmm hmm. Barrel racing school. Breeding racing horses. I have financing lined up. I just need to find the right land." The thought of all the work she had to do gave her heart a squeeze. Horses, staff, marketing. It seemed almost too much.

Garth rubbed his thumb on her forehead. "Why the worry lines?"

She relaxed. Tomorrow would be soon enough to embrace her anxiety. Tonight was for just them. "Lots to do."

He opened his mouth then closed it, running his palm up and down her side, over her hip and thigh, then back up to her ribs.

She waited patiently. He was not a man to be rushed. Well, except for tonight and her crazy idea of busting into his room and throwing a condom at him. And that had worked out exceptionally well.

"I've been thinking about this all evening." His jaw tightened and his brow furrowed. "Would you ever consider a partner?" His hand stopped on her hip. "Maybe adding a bullfighter school, too?"

Her eyes widened. Suddenly, she could see it clearly. Barrel racing one month, bullfighting the next. She sat up, staring blindly at the wall. She was the best in her sport. He was the best in his. They could pull in more students than they'd have room to house.

"Yes." She cupped her palms over her eyes, holding in a scream of excitement.

"Yes?" His voice sounded uncertain.

She turned to him, pressing her hands to his chest as she threw her leg over his hips and straddled him. "Yes. That would be amazing!" Her voice rose in speed and volume. "We're the best of the best, Garth. Together we'd make an unbeatable team."

"About financing the venture. I have a tidy sum saved."

"We'll have to involve lawyers and accountants to

figure that out, but I know we can make it profitable."
Wait, what had he said earlier? "You've been thinking about this? About us being partners?"

He nodded. "After you mentioned your business plan."

She crossed her arms and sat back, bumping her ass into his semi-hard cock. "*That's* what you were thinking about?" She held back a grin. "Not about how to get me into your bed?"

With amazing strength, he sat up and tugged her around until she was lying beneath him, her legs wrapped around his waist. "Sweetheart, I was beating myself up from the inside out for letting you go."

She bit her lip. "Really?" Wiggling her hips, she felt his staff harden against her thigh.

"Yeah, really. Before you showed up, I'd been trying to figure out where the night went wrong. How I could reverse time and not be such an idiot."

His admission sent happy tingles skidding around her heart. "No, you—"

He kissed her silent. "I have to apologize. I have my pride. When you talk about your degrees and your future plans, I felt like I could never be part of that."

"You can." She'd make sure he was.

He shifted and his hard cock bumped up against her pussy, making both of them groan. "Where the hell is that condom?"

She twisted sideways and pulled it out from under her. Circling her hips to tease his erection. "I haven't been with anyone for, oh, hell." She counted back. "Over six months. Clean bill of health."

"I'm clean, too, sweetheart, and it's been about that long for me, too." His eyes narrowed. "Since we started looking at each other closer." After rolling on the condom, he pressed his hips forward, sliding just the head of his cock into her slit.

She sighed, wanting him buried deep, but loving the topic of their conversation just as much. "Since we noticed that we'd make excellent lovers."

He pushed forward another inch, his cock penetrating deeper. Her slit tightened around him. He looked into her eyes. "Since you decided to take a chance on a rodeo bum."

"And you decided *not* to take a chance on a rich girl who you thought was too immature."

"I have some explaining to do about that. The age thing, I mean. It's a long, sad story, but I don't want to tackle it tonight." Pushing his hard-on into her, he groaned and shuddered.

"Um…" Her brain fogged over with desire. "Okay. Later." He had a perfect knack for making her forget what they were discussing.

Her body stretched and adjusted to fit him, her core vibrated with desire, and her mind started the slow spin towards climax.

Changing positions, his thighs spread her pussy farther open and he pressed his cock in until the last inches of his thick length drove into her, his heavy sack slapping against her.

Everything inside her tingled and sparked. Her hands found his strong shoulders, holding on like she was riding a runaway stallion.

His hips moved, pulling his shaft from her cunt then pumping it back in. His hands cupped her breasts and he groaned.

His touch flooded her chest with heat, her breasts swelled, and her nipples tightened to a lovely ache that skittered down into her core.

Bending his head, he kissed her breast, nipping and scraping his teeth along her flesh. When he sucked her nipple deep into her mouth, a tug sent her hips jerking, finding perfect rhythm with his slick strokes.

He took her other nipple into his mouth and teased it with his tongue. His fingers on her other breast plucked at her tight bud. The sensory overload turned her thoughts to slush as she raced toward the edge.

Garth moved his hand between their bodies and pinched her clit. Staring into her eyes, he demanded, "Come for me, Heather. Call my name."

"Garth!" she shouted as she leapt over top and sailed off into incredible pleasure. His hips jackhammered into her convulsing slit, his fingers plucked at her clit, the vibrations radiating up her body into her brain.

Pulsing beats of pure bliss traveled back down

into her body and tumbled her over and over in a wild, wicked ride.

His grunts signaled his own release and as she rolled slowly back to consciousness, she watched his face tighten into an expression of total bliss.

Kneeling between her legs, he held up her hips to take his cock and pumped into her, a primal beat that sent her heart racing, her soul crying with joy.

With his last, deep plunges, he shook and cried her name, guttural and base. When he collapsed, he lay mostly on the bed, partially on her, pressing her down under his hot body. His still-hard cock lay deep inside her still.

She didn't want to move. Ever.

His breathing came fast, his heart, beating against her ribs, pumped as wildly as hers. "Heather. You're everything I need."

Biting her lower lip, she sucked back a wave of happy tears. "I'm glad you finally realized it," she teased, but her voice held tender emotion.

He lifted up, propping his head on his bent arm. "Took me a while, huh?"

She brushed her fingers along his strong jaw. "We just needed to find the right motivator."

Turning his head, he kissed her hand. "And that was…?"

"A surprise dance in a dark forest?"

He laughed. "That was a surprise."

"I knew you couldn't resist me." She grinned and

wagged her brows at him. "Once you had me in your arms."

"Sweetheart," he growled, "If I'd have known how perfectly we fit together..." He turned her hips, withdrawing his shaft as he pushed back into her again, setting her body vibrating. His blue gaze locked with hers, a sheen of emotion clouding them. "I'd have danced *every* dance with you."

"Garth." Her voice choked on a swell of tears. "Remember those fifty years you'd already planned out for us?" Heather sucked in an uneven breath and ran her fingers through his wild mop of hair. "I'm willing to give you that long to make it up to me."

~ ~ ~ ~

Where We Left Off

"Oh, Cookie Dough, why'd you choose today to have a breach birth?" Veterinarian Taylor Kershaw knelt next to her little brown and white mare. Taylor's pink shirt and blue jeans were soaked from trudging to the barn without grabbing a coat. They clung to her curvy body like a wet t-shirt contest.

Lying on her side in the hay, the horse labored to push. Her groan cut through Taylor like a knife. This had been going on too long. She needed to help Cookie Dough deliver the foal, but it was a two-person job.

Standing, she walked to the barn door and cracked it open. Snow blew in, borne on the howling wind of the late spring storm. Another inch had accumulated since she'd come out to the barn a half hour ago. She'd been alerted by Cookie Dough's cries through the baby monitor she'd left near the horse's stall. The roads had been impassable for nearly four hours. "When will this end?"

Cookie Dough vocalized in her stall. Taylor shut the door and went back to her. "Okay, baby girl. I'll see if I can get some help." There was only one person close enough to get here in time. She'd sworn never to talk to the man again, but to save the mare and foal, she'd do just about anything. Hell, she'd get down on her knees and beg. Picking up the barn phone, she called information. "Can you connect me with Duke Leading? He's a veterinarian. I need his emergency number."

411 put her directly through.

"Dr. Leading." His voice rumbled, low and confident.

"It's Taylor Kershaw."

Silence.

"Hello?" Oh, God, had the line gone dead?

"Dr. Kershaw." He sounded both surprised and sexy. How did he always do that?

"I need your help." She nearly choked as she swallowed her pride.

"My help?" A short, humorless laugh burst through the phone. "You've been stealing my customers, undercutting my rates, advertising—"

"Please." Here was the begging part. "I can't do this alone, and my ranch hand is stranded in town."

"You're serious?" His voice turned professional. "What's going on?"

"I took in a rescue mare. She's been in labor for maybe thirty minutes. The foal is breech, but I can't pull it out myself." Tears flooded her eyes. She couldn't lose the little horse. Not after nursing her back to health for six months and falling hoof-over-halter in love with her. "Is there any way you can get here?"

"Hang on, Taylor. I'll be there." The line went dead.

With a sense of relief that bordered on dizziness, she hung up the receiver and walked into Cooke Dough's stall. The horse's big brown eyes looked at her, pleading. "Help is on the way, sweet girl. You just take it easy." She checked her again. Should she try standing her up to see if she could reposition the foal?

The horse wasn't straining yet. She would wait. But what if Duke couldn't get through? Their ranches were adjacent, their houses relatively close, but still it was nearly a mile between them.

Which was always the most maddening irony of the whole stinking situation.

She'd turned the barn lights down to prepare for the birth. Rummaging through the tack room, she found a trouble light and brought it to the stall, just in case.

Sooner than she expected, the big barn door opener started rumbling. Peeking over the stall, she saw Duke ride in on a huge draft horse. Both the man and the animal were nearly covered with sticky, white snow.

She jogged over and closed the barn door as he dismounted and shook a small mound of snow off his clothes. When she reached for the horse's reins, he held up a hand. "Conan's okay for now. Let's take a look at your mare." He peeled off his gloves and set them by the radiator. Next came his long, black duster, which he hung on a peg in the wall, his cowboy hat beside it.

He turned toward her, flexing his fingers, his whole body shivering. "Cold out there."

Relief and gratitude flowed through her and that tingly burning wet her eyes. "Thank you for coming." This time, it didn't require any pride swallowing.

Duke's face was red where his thick brown scruff didn't cover. He ran his fingers through his curly, collar-length hair, flinging snow clumps from the ends. He stepped closer. Looking down at her from his six feet six inches, his chocolate brown eyes pierced her. "I'm glad you called me."

An ache landed like a rock in her heart. They could have been so good together. Two years ago, things had been escalating between them, the sexual tension crackling like static electricity. Then all hell had broken loose followed by his damn stubborn insistence that they change the focus of their practice… No. This wasn't the time for anger. She had to concentrate on Cookie Dough. Turning, she walked to the stall. "I've had her up a couple times. Reached in and felt the hocks. The legs are positioned correctly. She just can't push her baby out. And I'm not strong enough to pull."

Duke stepped into the stall and sat on his heels by Cookie Dough's head. "Hi, little lady. I'm here to help." He let her smell his palms and breath, and ran a calming hand over her nose and neck. "She's young."

"Too young. They bred her too early." Petting the

mare's distended belly, she added, "She was in bad shape when I got her."

Duke looked up at her, anger in his eyes. "Did they get the bastards?"

She nodded. "They're in jail."

He ran his hands over the scars on the mare's shoulder. "Poor gal."

Taylor knew how calming and tender Duke's hands could be. Before their partnership fell apart, he'd held her, comforted her when her father died. But they'd never kissed. Even though a roaring fire ignited every time they got close to each other, they'd taken it slow for the sake of their business. A lot of good that did.

Duke stood and went to Cookie Dough's hind end. He sat on his heels again. His Carhartt bibs were wet from the knees down, his cowboy boots dripping.

"I've got some big coveralls if you want to change."

He stood. "And a place to wash up?" Duke looked at her, his gaze raking down her body, pausing at her breasts, her waist, then following her legs. "You're soaked."

A shiver rattled her bones. Was it from her cold clothes, or his appraisal? "I need to change, too."

Taylor preceded him to the tack room. She took down a pair of her ranch hand's coveralls and handed them to Duke. Choosing an old but clean sky-blue jumpsuit for herself—the one her father had said matched her eyes—she stepped into the office, out of view of the man who could still turn her desperately horny with just one look. After stripping down to her bra and panties and changing into the coveralls, she pinned her long, brown braids on her head, out of her way. "Decent?" she called.

"Always," he replied.

Still completely dressed, he was texting from his phone. He glanced at her and smiled. "I forgot to tell my foreman I was taking off."

She sighed. He'd left his warm home, braved a blizzard, just to come to her.

His eyebrows drew down. "What?"

Taylor shook her head. "Nothing." At the sink, she scrubbed her hands and watched as he peeled off his bibs. "I can those. I'll hang them by the radiator to dry off." She dried her hands. "You should take off your shirt and pants, too."

He glanced at her, his eyebrow shooting up. "Oh yeah?"

Taylor felt a blush climb her cheeks. "Her amniotic sac hasn't broken yet."

She opened a cabinet and took out a pair of rubber boots. "You can use these, if you want."

He stood in his jeans. Giving her a grin, his hand moved to his waist. His belt buckle clinked and his zipper buzzed.

She grabbed his Carhartts and headed for the door. She couldn't help but wonder—boxers or briefs? She peeked. Black boxer briefs snugged his big, muscular thighs and showed off his very tight ass. God, he looked good. She'd seen him a number of times over the years, but always at a distance. She'd avoided him as diligently as he'd avoided her.

As she walked toward the radiator, the warmth of his heavy pants in her arms, along with the musky smell of a horse-riding man wafted up to her nose. She gave in to the temptation and took a deep sniff. She missed Duke. They'd grown close as she'd spent those first years of her veterinary career learning from him.

She hated what had happened to them since.

The clomp of rubber boots sounded and she quickly hung up his bibs. He dropped his cowboy boots next to the stove. "Ready?"

She turned toward him and smiled at the blaze orange outfit that was a furlong too short in both the arms and legs.

Grinning, he held out his arms, making the sleeves go even shorter. "Not my favorite color, but as long as you don't take any pictures…"

She lifted her brows. He seemed different, more relaxed. "For my next advertising campaign?" she teased.

The smile left his face. "We *will* talk about that. After."

Damn. She'd been afraid of that. Taylor glanced down. She'd been aggressive as she built her practice, but she'd rationalized it. Told herself it was just business. Today, Duke risked his life getting here, no questions asked—he just came when she'd called. It was more than "just business." To both of them.

They entered the stall and all thoughts faded away except for the health of Cookie Dough and her foal.

Working together with the horse's contractions, they tugged, pulled, and eased a beautiful brown and white colt from the mare. While momma and baby boy rested with the umbilical cord still intact, Taylor sat on a hay bale outside the stall watching them bond. After Duke unsaddled Conan, brushed him down, and set him up in a stall, he joined Taylor on the bale.

"Isn't it just a tiny miracle?" she said quietly.

"It's always amazing to me. Whether it's a horse or a cow or a chicken."

She grinned. "A chicken?"

He shrugged. "I have chickens now, over at the ranch. I get my thrills watching them hatch."

Taylor stifled a laugh, not wanting to startle the horses. "I never knew you were that domestic."

"I've learned to enjoy the little things in life." He shook his head. "I name them, too."

"The chickens?" He *had* changed. He used to be intense, focused. Driven to have everything perfect—and "perfect" meant "his way."

"Yep. I've gotten pretty good at it, too."

"Let's put your skill to the test." She gestured

toward the stall. "Pick a name for the colt."

He held up his hands. "Oh, no. You don't want a chicken name for that handsome stud. I'd come up with something dopey like..." He furrowed his brows in concentration.

"Cookie Dough?"

He laughed. "Yeah, Cookie Dough." Glancing at the horse, he said, "Beautiful horse. But dumbest name ever."

She pursed her lips, feigning anger. "I. Named. Her."

His gaze shot to her face. "Really?"

A smile parted her lips. "Really." She sighed. "While sitting on this bale eating cookie dough ice cream. It was the night I brought her home. I didn't know if she'd live or die." The threat of a sob closed her airway and she quickly pushed it away. "And look at her now." Her voice wavered.

Duke took her hand and held it tight in his.

His warmth, his kindness swelled that place in her heart that had been shriveled and dry since they'd said goodbye two years ago.

They sat in thoughtful silence for a long time, their shoulders touching, watching the horses. Duke told a couple stories of unexpected breech births, and she shared a few of her own.

Cookie Dough turned out to be a good mother, even at her young age. Within fifteen minutes, she stood and began caring for her baby.

Duke waited on the bale as Taylor checked the foal and helped clean him.

She came out of the stall and quietly closed the gate. Leaning on it, she watched the horses, so relieved she could cry. Again.

He walked up next to her. "Big foal. Probably 90 pounds."

"No wonder she couldn't push her out alone." Taylor looked up at him. "Thanks, Duke. I really appreciate your help." The wind howled and banged something up against the barn. "You're welcome to stay the night."

"I'm planning on it." He stared at her for a moment. His gaze lifted to her hair and he picked out a piece of hay. "I can sleep in the barn, if you'd like."

How could she let him stay in the barn after he'd braved a blizzard to help her? "There's plenty of room in the house." She immediately wished she could call back those words. If he were down the hall in her guest room, how would she be able to resist temptation?

"Are you still..." He glanced away, then stared into her eyes. "Are you seeing anyone?"

A thrill of pure sensual awareness raced through her, starting her heart beating faster and warming her deep inside her belly. "No. Are you?"

He gave her a spare smile. "No."

That familiar smile, the reminder of how things had been between them, caught her up in memories.

"How did we go so wrong, Duke?"

"We were so damn worried about the business." He leaned his forearms on top of the gate. "Wanting to keep it professional, making sure your dad didn't notice the chemistry between us."

"You're right." She shrugged. "Looking back, it all seems pointless. The fighting. The bitterness of the last two years."

"Has it been that long?" His voice trailed off.

"Are you still..." Should she bring up a touchy subject? He'd warned her he wanted to talk about it. Might as well dive in. "Are you still planning to open an office in town?"

He turned toward her, leaning sideways on the gate. "I'd like to. The housing project out past the railroad tracks should be finished this summer. Lots of people with pets who need veterinary care."

Taylor crossed her arms. "I'm sorry I shot down your idea, Duke. It makes a great deal of sense to me now. Combining large and small animal care would increase your client base incrementally."

"Actually," he laughed. "It makes sense *now*, with the additional housing going in." He looked down and shuffled his rubber boot. "But two years ago? It probably would have failed."

Her eyes opened wide. Was this Duke saying he'd been wrong?

His crooked grin flashed. "Yeah. You were right to shoot it down back then."

Back then. "What about now?"

"I could do it, but I'd need a partner."

Warmth settled around her heart. Partners. All through vet school, she'd dreamed of being his partner. During her internship with him, dreamed of the two of them sharing a business. Sharing a life.

"Do you have anyone in mind?" She pulled a silly smile.

Sliding his hand up her arm to her neck, he nodded. "Just one perfectly obstinate, amazingly wonderful woman."

Taylor laid her hands on his hard chest, a blast of tenderness choking her. "No way you're talking about me."

He chuckled then sobered. "I've missed you, Taylor. Missed working with you. Just talking with you." He stroked his fingertips over her cheek. "Touching you." His voice quieted.

A tremor of profound longing shook her. "I've missed you, too."

Duke slid his hand to the nape of her neck. His other hand pressed against her lower back, pulling her close. His eyes took on a dangerous gleam. "What the hell were we thinking back them?"

"We should have…" What? Gone for it? Become lovers and hoped everything else fell into place?

His face was an inch from hers. A look that might have been anger darkened his eyes. "What we should have done, was this." His lips molded to hers, firm and warm. His tongue played along her lips, enticing her to open for him.

With a sigh, she parted her lips. A shiver raced across her skin, puckering her nipples. This was Duke kissing her. Finally, after all these years, after all the nights she'd dreamt of this moment.

His tongue cradled hers, skimmed it, and drew it into his own mouth. He tasted like coffee, his permanent addiction. With a growl, he deepened the kiss, pulled her tighter against him, pressed his erection into her belly.

Her core heated and jittered as she arched her back, moving tighter against his stiff cock. Her hand slipped upward to the zipper pull on the overalls. Was she brave enough?

Duke moved his lips a fraction of an inch from hers. "Show me you want this, Taylor." His eyes ranged over her face, desperation, desire filling his gaze.

Inching the pull downward, she let the buzz of his zipper ramble through her brain. She'd have him naked. Finally. It was almost surreal.

His hand at the nape of her neck moved to her hair. After unfastening the clip that held her braids, he tugged out the bands at the bottom.

Taylor bared his chest and ran her fingers through the soft mat of fur.

Duke unraveled her pigtails and combed his fingers through them. "I love your hair." He grinned.

"I like it long." He wrapped her hair around his fist and gently tipped her head back. "And loose." The fingers of his other hand trailed from her jaw down to her zipper pull. "I've wanted you for four years, Taylor." He eased down the pull. "Since the day I met you, I had a craving for you."

His words flowed through her like melted chocolate, swelling her breasts, heating her core, and sending wicked tingles through her pussy lips. Pressing her thighs together, she let the desire build in her, let it overtake her.

When he'd unzipped past her waist, he slid the fabric off her shoulders. His gaze fastened on her breasts. His hand moved to her bra strap.

She shivered as her nipples puckered, imagining his tongue licking her, sucking her peaks deep into his mouth.

"You're cold." He pulled the shoulders of her coverall back up and tugged the fabric together over her breasts.

"N…no." She swallowed and blinked herself out of her sensual haze. "Not cold."

He chuckled. "Hard to talk?"

She looked up into his eyes. "You're a tease."

"Woman, I mean to tease *and* please." He looked at the stall where the two horses stood close together. "We need to stay out here 'till she drops the placenta." He looked around and grinned. "Wait here." Pulling a big hay bale along the barn floor, he positioned it close to the radiator.

Taylor smiled. She hadn't done it in a barn since high school.

He dragged another big bale and shoved it behind the first one, then grabbed another and set it on top of the second, creating a set of steps facing the radiator.

He stood, looking at her, not even breathing hard from his exertion. "Come over here, woman."

Years ago, he called her that when they were alone. She'd tell him to stop flirting. She wished she never had. If they'd been intimate back then, if they'd given in to their hearts, maybe things would have worked out for the business. And for them.

She walked into his arms. The hay bales served to capture the warmth of the radiator.

Duke tugged her coverall off one shoulder and bent his head to her neck. Nibbling, he ran a line down her shoulder, back up to her neck, and up to her ear. Grabbing her earlobe between his teeth, he bit gently.

Each touch of his mouth spun her deeper into a sensual vortex. As he eased her bra strap down, she wished she'd worn something sexier than her plain white cotton.

He peeled down her coverall and unfastened her bra in a fast, wild gesture, letting her jumper hang from her waist, and tossing her bra aside.

His eyes darkened and his breath sped as he stared at her breasts. "Unreal." He glanced into her eyes.

then down again. "You are spectacular, woman." He bent and took one nipple into his mouth while holding her other breast in his big hand.

She gripped his shoulder and let her head drop back. Her hair tickled as it curtained down her spine.

When his mouth turned greedy, sucking her deep, circling her nipple, she cried out. Her pussy quivered, wet and swollen, as each tug of his lips blasted hot flares into her core.

He moved to her other nipple, nibbling, stirring a whole new set of lush twinges convulsing in her slit. Her knees weakened and he caught her by the hips. "I want to lay you down, Taylor." His gaze burned into hers. "I'm going to feast on you until you go crazy."

Sucking in a breath, she let his words drive her mad. "I want you, Doc." She used her pet name for him, loving the feeling that the past years of separation made no difference.

Holding her upright, he steadied her while he grabbed his duster from the wall. Laying it over the top hay bale, he picked her up and stood her on the lower bale.

Looking down at him as he stood on the floor, she sought the words to tell him how much he meant to her. How she'd missed him, and how it had all come back the moment he rode through her barn door today. Her hero.

The moment was lost as he eased her coveralls lower on her hips and kissed her belly.

"Oh, God." She'd give anything to have his mouth down low. Kissing her pussy, fucking her with his tongue and his fingers.

Slowly he tugged her jumpsuit and panties down, seductively revealing her trimmed pussy. He bared her thighs, then her legs and feet as he disposed of her clothes and shoes.

Duke kissed her kneecap, looked up at her with a grin that would rival a devil's, and licked his way from her knee to her pussy.

An electric charge raced through Taylor, pinging to each nerve ending in her body. He took her waist in his hands and eased her back to sit on the top bale, on the dry warmth of his duster. "Lay back, Taylor." He spread her legs and knelt on the lower bale, between her feet.

She leaned back on her elbows but couldn't look away from his face. His breath panted through his parted lips as he stared at her mound, ran his hands up and down her thighs, his rough skin a sensual delight. His eyelids drooped, hooding his dark irises.

A wild streak of lust raced through her, converging in her slit. Unable to hold herself up, she collapsed back on his coat.

"That's what I like," he murmured. "I want you spread out for me, open and wet."

A small cry left her lips as she closed her eyes and silently begged him to taste her.

He did. With a growl, his lips met her pussy,

kissing and nibbling, moving down then back up to her opening, where his tongue explored, circled, licked until she couldn't stand it.

Sliding her hand down her body, she parted her lips with her fingers and touched her clit.

"No, Taylor." He laughed, wicked and low. He took her finger in his mouth and sucked it. "You have to learn to be patient."

"You know I'm not a patient woman." She grabbed his hair and put his mouth where she wanted it.

Her entire body jolted as his lips touched her clit.

Wrapping his arms under her thighs, he moved her legs onto his shoulders. His hand on her ass held her pussy up to his mouth.

His other arm reached up and cupped her breast. His index finger twisted around her nipple in a pattern so ingenious, she could come any second just from the pleasure. He dove in, his mouth open, tongue out, sliding up and down her cunt.

It felt like every inch of her flamed then cooled only to instantly flame again. When his lips clasped onto her clit and sucked, she was lost.

Spinning, she dropped her head down over the back of the bale as the world tumbled off its axis and twirled wildly. Swirls of bliss raced up and down her spine, her flesh heated and sensitized, tingling over every inch. A moan escaped her lips as pure paradise separated her from her body for a long moment.

As the world righted itself, her body and mind reconnected, Duke licked her along her heated slit and kissed her thighs.

She opened her eyes and turned her head to check on the new arrival. Momma and baby stood close together.

His hands left her. His footstep headed away then back again.

Lifting her head with the last of her strength, Taylor saw Duke digging in the pocket of his jeans. Was he leaving? She sat up, blinking to clear her vision.

He held up a foil packet. A condom.

"You come prepared for everything, don't you." She sat up.

"I'd hoped we'd have a chance to reconcile." He hung his jeans and walked over to her.

Taylor stood on the lower bale, looking down into his face.

He pulled her close, kissing her lips, then her breasts. "You're amazing, Taylor. If I didn't have this desperation to be inside you right now, I'd do that again. Twice."

Tunneling her fingers through his hair, she sighed. "I don't think *I* could do it again. Even once. That was life altering." She kissed the top of his head, smelling his woodsy shampoo.

He chuckled as he nuzzled between her breasts. "Glad I pleased you."

Taylor reached down and unzipped his coveralls. "It's my turn to please *you.*" Pulling the cloth from his shoulders, she knelt on the bale to shove them down his legs. Met with an impressive rise in those sexy black briefs, she stopped and put her hand over his hot length.

His shudder told her he liked it. When she looked up into his eyes, his dark gaze bore into hers. "Taylor." His voice rolled, low and intense. "I want to take you, woman."

Quivering started in her recently satisfied core, rekindling the fire and reigniting her desire.

Peeling off his briefs, she let them drop and wrapped her hand around his thick cock. "Hot," she whispered as she kissed the head, tasting his creamy pre-cum.

His body jerked and a muted moan broke from his throat.

Taylor slid her lips over his head and twirled her tongue around the rim.

"Uh uh." Duke's hands were on her shoulders, pushing her back. "That was really good. But save it for later." He eased her up to stand on the bale and jumped up beside her. "Right now, I have to be inside you, Taylor." As he rolled on the condom, his thick cock pulsed with desire. He caught her arms, pulling her close.

His kiss demanded everything from her. She barely felt her hands rubbing up and down his thighs, his chest, his stomach. His tongue tasted every crevice of her mouth, then hers did the same, loving the desperation in his tight hold, his fiery kiss.

He grabbed her ass and hiked her up. "Wrap your legs around me." His voice was a growl.

She gladly obeyed, holding onto his shoulders. Feeling his hard shaft poised at her opening, she adjusted herself for what she knew would come next. She needed this more than anything. His erection inside her.

"I want you. Now." He let her slide down until his cock eased into her, filling her and jittering her core with spikes of pleasure.

Duke's jaw clenched as he uttered a broken curse. He stepped back and sat on his duster on the top bale. His body tensed and his hands lifted her hips, sliding nearly completely out of her, then back in again with more power.

She unwrapped her legs and knelt, spread across his lap, his thick, fiery staff throbbing inside her. Gently she pushed him. "Lay back, cowboy." She smiled seductively. "Let me do the work."

He grabbed her hair and possessed her mouth with his, frantic desire making the kiss rough and quick. Releasing her mouth, releasing her hair, he eased back onto his elbows, watching her with dark eyes that sparked with lust, and breath that heaved in and out of his chest.

Taylor arched her back, easing his erection deeper

inside her pussy. Raging pleasure stole through her and she cried out wordlessly. Rotating her pelvis, she stared into his eyes, loving the animal passion in him that was desperate for release.

Her body shivered with the control she held over him. Quickening her movements, she laid her hands on his chest and dropped her head forward. Her hair cascaded over her arms to lay on his chest and abdomen.

With a groan, he lay back, running his fingers through her hair. "Soft." His eyes closed and he rubbed her baby-fine locks between his fingers then over his chest. He'd always commented on her hair. Now she knew why.

The angle of his cock hit her just right and a building flood of bliss grew inside her. The artful dance of her hips changed to match her growing desire for release. Sliding her channel up and down his heavy staff, she let her movements become primal, sharp. Soon, she rode him at a full gallop, throwing back her head.

His hands cupped her breasts, his fingers tugging at her nipples, sending explosions of pleasure deep into her pussy.

Reaching back, she grasped his balls and gave a soft tug, making him roar and bare his teeth.

Her world began to shatter, and when his hand touched her mound and quickly found her clit, she cried in ecstasy.

His hips slammed up as hers drove down, thrusting his shaft deep, hard, fast, until they both shouted. She flew into a million pieces, pinpoints of light suffusing her brain, pulsing and sparking. Her mind crumbled in a delight so overwhelming, she didn't know if she'd find her way back.

Duke's pumping slowed but the friction of him inside her kept her in pieces. Each time she got closer to reality, his thumb on her clit created tiny cracks that sent her breaking away again.

When she collapsed onto his chest, he wrapped his arms tightly around her, kissing the top of her head, her temple, her cheek.

Under her ear, his heart raced full speed, his breath pumped in and out of his lungs.

"Duke." She slid her hands over his muscled shoulders, down his big, hard arms. "That was wonderful."

"Yeah." He ran a hand down her hair, along her spine. "You are spectacular."

She giggled a little. "My pleasure." Stacking her hands on his clavicle, she propped her chin on them. "Can we do it again?"

He laughed and wiggled his hips. "Soon. Very soon." His cock lay inside her pussy, still mostly hard.

She eased him out of her slit and lay next to him on the bale, her head on his shoulder. "If Cookie Dough dropped her placenta, we can go try it in the house."

He ran his hand down her arm and tugged her closer. His smile was silly. "I don't know. We're vets. Shouldn't we prefer doing it in a barn?"

"Doing it," she murmured, not for any reason, just because it sounded funny.

He pulled back. His face turned serious. "That was the wrong thing to say, Taylor. We weren't just doing it, we made love."

Her breath caught in her throat. "Did we?"

"You know we did." He tucked a strand of her hair behind her ear. "We took a wrong turn somewhere about two years ago, and if I could turn back time, I'd—"

Taylor touched a finger to his lips. "I know we have a lot to talk about, but not tonight, okay?" She traced the strong line of his jaw. "We've found a good place to start over from."

He nipped at her finger. "On top of a hay bale?"

She laughed. "Yes, that, too. But if my dad hadn't died, this…our making love…would have happened sooner, rather than later."

"Maybe if it had…" He cupped her cheek and stared into her eyes. "Things wouldn't have gone so far sideways."

"I've been thinking the same thing." When she remembered all the arguments and misunderstandings, then the two years of complete silence, her heart ached. "We can fix it."

He nodded, a cocky smile curved his lips. "I'll make sure we do, woman." He paused, and his smile left him. "My woman."

Something in her chest skittered, both at hearing his words, and at the intense look in his eyes.

Cookie Dough whinnied and stomped. Taylor sat up to see the foal at his mother's teat. "The colt is nursing."

Duke sat next to her, his arm around her shoulders. "Ain't that the most beautiful site in the world?"

"It truly is." She sighed and snuggled in. "And we owe this..." She kissed him, quickly and tenderly. "...all to her."

His smile lit his face. "I know how we can thank her."

"Oh yeah? How?"

"Let's name our firstborn after her."

Taylor gave in to joyous laughter and a few rogue tears. Her heart swelled with the realization that their future had been restored by one sweet little mare.

~~~~
~~~~

Connect With Me

Thank you for reading my stories. I hope you enjoyed reading them as much as I liked writing them. I'd love to hear which cowboy was your favorite and why. Send me an e-mail at Randi@RandiAlexander.com, or connect with me through one of the sites listed below.

All my best,

Randi

"Rode Hard and Put Up Satisfied"

Website:
http://RandiAlexander.com
Facebook:
https://www.facebook.com/RandiAlexanderAuthor
Twitter:
https://twitter.com/#!/Randi_Alexander
Goodreads:
http://www.goodreads.com/author/show/4885056.Randi_Alexander
Wild and Wicked Cowboys Blog:
http://wildandwickedcowboys.wordpress.com/

Need more cowboys? Stop by my website to read the first chapters, watch the video trailers, and read reviews of my other books:

Other Books by Randi Alexander

Available Now at http://www.WilderRoses.com/:

Chase and Seduction - Country music superstar/actor Chase Tanner has yet to be denied anything—and he's never wanted anything or anyone more than gorgeous screenplay writer Reno Linden. So when the film they are working on is finally finished, Chase decides to turn up the volume on seducing Reno.

Reno Linden lived a quiet, rural life until she was thrust into the Hollywood scene when her book was adapted to film. Chase Tanner is larger than life, sinfully sexy and hell-bent on getting her into bed. Skittish after a failed wedding engagement, Reno risks the plunge into Chase's arms, and is surprised that her good girl self can keep up with bad boy Chase.

Though Chase returns to his cowboy roots often, and Reno cherishes the time spent with him on his ranch, the two find their careers pulling them in different directions. Will their attraction survive the glitz and stress of fame?

Her Cowboy Stud - Trace McGonagall's quiet life on his Houston stud ranch is shaken up when gorgeous Macy Veralta arrives to claim an inheritance left to her in his uncle's will. Trace sees her as just another gold digger, but he also can't resist her curvy body. When she hints at being the perfect submissive to his Dom, he has to have her.

Macy wouldn't have been three months late to claim her inheritance if she'd known Trace was sin in jeans. The cowboy's dominant bearing and the smoldering glint in his eyes send shivers to her toes and stirs images of being bound in his bed and disciplined at his hand. But could Trace's perfect seduction be part of his plan to reclaim her inheritance?

Available For Preorder at http://www.Amazon.com/:

Banging the Cowboy (short story in the Cowboy Lust anthology) - Every Saturday for a year, Annie Paris has lusted after Rafe McCord from behind her drumset on stage at the honky tonk. The Big Cowboy, they call him, and rumors say he likes it rough in the bedroom. The thought of banging him makes Annie's pussy tingle and cream.

But Rafe is a one-night-stand kind of guy, and Annie couldn't handle seeing him every Saturday, knowing she'd already had her one night with him. That there'd be no more.

Tonight, something's different. Rafe doesn't leave with a woman. And he's been staring at Annie since he came in the door. At closing time, he sets his longneck on the bar, and swaggers toward her, his gaze locked on hers, his smile pure sexual invitation. Annie's slit contracts and her nipples harden. Oh, God, if he asks her to his house for a rough ride on his big, hard cock, where would she find the strength to say "no"?

Coming Soon:

Turn Up the Heat - During the filming of the reality show America's Newest Chef, finalist Mackenzie Jarvis falls desperately in lust with actress Gina Volto. Mackenzie's never been with a woman, and her strict Wyoming upbringing has her questioning whether she can loosen up enough to live out her fantasy.

When Gina shows Mackenzie how sensual their nights could be, Mackenzie ignores her doubts for one wild weekend. Monday morning, she returns home to her ranch, her horses, and her busy career as the owner and chef of a restaurant. But a week later Gina shows up at Mackenzie's home. She's come to Wyoming-for Mackenzie.

Gina teaches Mackenzie the sweet pleasures of loving a woman, the naughty sting of a whip, and the seductive submission of bondage. But Gina admits she wants more than just a few days. Can conservative, family-valued Mackenzie ignore the plans she's made for her life, and find her future in the tender arms of a woman?

About the Author

Randi Alexander is published with The Wild Rose Press Cowboy Kink line. When she's not dreaming of, or writing about, kinky cowboys, she's biking trails along remote rivers, snorkeling the Gulf of Mexico, or practicing her drumming in hopes of someday forming a tropical-rock band.

Romance novels have been Randi's hideout since she was a teen. The chance to imagine herself as the strong but vulnerable heroine, and the guarantee of a "Happily Ever After" ending, have always been irresistible.

Erotic romance is her newest passion. It still lets her live the heroine's life and gives her a lovely ending, but also allows her to witness the attraction between the characters as they explore physical love. She hopes her writing sweeps you away and grants you pleasant dreams of all your fantasies coming true.